THE BANDIT'S REDEMPTION

OUTLAW HEARTS SERIES

BOOK ONE

KYLEE WOODLEY

WILD HEART BOOKS

ISBN-13: 978-1-963212-18-1

To Monty, because you taught me to dream.

CHAPTER 1

MARCH 1875
LOS ANGELES, CALIFORNIA

*A*t last, it had come! Jesse Alexander slid a finger across the mahogany side of the American Optical Compact View Camera Box. Shipped fresh from New York City. His older sister, Aubrey, would love it! He settled the box on a tripod he had set up before the open window in his study and unlatched the brass guides. They swung down, allowing the slide holder to come back and straighten out the tapering bellows. Jesse pointed the camera out the window. He draped the black sash over his head and the box to peer through the lens.

Through the window, green and blue mixed together in a haze. He adjusted the bellows, and lights yielded to details. In a yard of lush green grass, near resplendent pink rose bushes, stood Aubrey in a nondescript dress, shoulders stooped and chin tucked to her chest. When she turned, gaze vague, the blue sky seemed to grow darker.

Nothing had been the same since Jesse fetched her home from Utah that past December. Aubrey had never told him what sent her into the dormant moods. Jesse suspected the worst, and his stomach turned at the thought. Might Aubrey's love of photography bring her back to herself?

"Jess?" Pa spoke behind him, tugging off the fabric and tossing it aside. "Still playing with your toys, I see."

Heat sped into his cheeks, though the irritation in Pa's expression faded when he glanced through the window to Aubrey. "Time. Safety and time are what she needs."

Jesse wasn't so sure. After all, he'd seen people wallow in their misery so long they seemed to grow comfortable in it. Aubrey needed something more. She needed a reason to live, smile, and enjoy the world around her.

"I just heard from my foreman at the Placerville Mine." Pa tugged his suit coat closed, buttoning it, then crossing his arms. "He said a neighboring mine had claim jumpers. Some of their men were killed. I'm leaving for Placerville tomorrow, and you're going to Cariboo Mountain."

Jesse stifled a groan. "Abe Johnson is better suited for the job and—"

"You are my son." Pa's words resounded off the wood-panel walls despite the carpet which should have softened the effect. Red crept up Pa's neck, and he stuck out his chin—a dare in his eyes.

They'd traveled this route before and found anger and disappointment at the end.

But Pa was wrong. "Who better to rule a kingdom, the noble born or a wise patriot who loves his country?"

"Jess..." Pa massaged the bridge of his nose.

"Who better to forge iron, the blacksmith's son or his apprentice? Whose garden returns the greatest harvest, he who knows the soil, the seasons, the plants, or he who owns the ground? Pa, just because I am born to—"

"You are born to this life, to my fortune."

"But I am not best suited to tend it."

"You are my son," came the usual retort, as though it settled all.

"This is a matter of poor stewardship, Pa. Abe will do the job better. With him in charge, you would run less risk of losing money and loss of lives for the workers. I am no miner. How will you govern the fortune God has given you if you choose your son over one more capable?"

Pa gripped his shoulders. "The fortune will be yours some day when I am gone. You can appoint whomever you want then."

"Respectfully, sir, why not delegate the responsibility now and spare yourself the loss and me the burden?"

"Because, Jess, the burden is yours to carry. If you are to be responsible for the lives of our miners, the fortunes of their families, and future generations, you need to know the burden now when I am here to help you carry it."

Losing the upper hand on reason, Jesse ground his teeth. He stared out the window, only to find Aubrey closer. Dark rings framed her eyes. His likely wore a similar shadow since he had sat with her every night, reading. What would she do when Jesse was gone? Unable to stoke the fire and read away her ghosts?

"What about Aubrey?" He faced his father, whom he'd outgrown in height years ago.

Although Titus Alexander was bigger than Jesse in more ways than his broad shoulders, he seemed to wilt when he looked at his daughter. "Your aunt will come to stay with her while we are gone."

"We can't just leave her."

"What good have we been to her, both home this snowy season while the mines are closed?"

Jaw aching, Jesse shook his head. He hated this, being torn between Pa's demands and what he knew was right. He needed to take a stand. "It just feels wrong, Pa," he finally managed to say when his reasoning gave way to despair. After all, Pa had already formed his argument so well.

"Feelings, son, cannot be trusted. Better to trust reason, doing what is right for the sake of right. A man's code of honor is what he has to fall back on when every road around him seems to lead nowhere. Aubrey has had her time." The creaking of floorboards in the hall brought Pa's voice to a hush, though he managed his final statement before turning. "If she was going to come back to herself, she would have by now."

The door to Jesse's study whispered open, and in stepped his lovely, pale-skinned sister.

"Aubrey?" Pa turned, his voice warm when he greeted her with the typical peck to her forehead. "Amuse your brother. He has a new toy."

The room fell silent on Pa's exit. Jesse scooped up the black material Pa had discarded onto the floor and folded it. "Toy," he murmured. Here he was surrounded by his beloved books— the poetry, atlases, novels, proverbs—where he had buried himself when Aubrey left and Ma died. It was his sanctuary, but he'd always known Pa would drag him from it, thrusting manly duty at his feet. He'd once reveled at the chance to prove himself, but not anymore.

"An American Optical?" Aubrey touched the brass lens where the inscription read, *Freedom*.

He stepped nearer the large box. "Yes, their latest model. The tapered bellows allow for a clearer photograph."

She peered into the screen, though she would not see anything without the scarf to block out all light except what poured through the front lens. Jesse draped the black fabric over her head. She adjusted the bellows.

Did she feel like her old self, viewing something beautiful, meant to be captured to relive the moment when time had passed?

Aubrey straightened, pulling the fabric from her head to

give to him. She cupped the corner of the box and ran a finger along the edge. "I have never seen one so large. What do you hope to capture with this?"

"Something special." He grinned, and she cocked her head to the side. "Do you remember the lake we would stop by on our trips to Cariboo Mountain?"

Her eyes widened. "You are going to take a photo of Grays Lake with this big thing?"

Jesse folded the black fabric neatly, placing it on top. "Yep."

Aubrey turned away, dismissively.

"You don't think I can do it?"

She shrugged.

"Let's make a deal—if I capture the entire lake clearly, you have to do something for me."

"What?"

"A trip to Europe. You always wanted to go abroad."

She glanced down, her shoulders stooped. "I don't know, Jess. That was a long time ago."

"We can go together and visit *Grandmere* in France."

"If you can even capture the lake."

He rocked on his heels and wagged his eyebrows.

Aubrey waved him away with a flitter of her hand.

"Our deal?"

She nodded, then moved from sight.

Jesse drew in a deep breath, turning to the desk, and shifted about the papers he had there. How was he going to manage being away from Aubrey? If he could get that photograph, she would agree to go with him abroad. He just needed to get her out of the house for her to return to herself. He turned a newspaper over to read the small article he'd noticed just before the camera was delivered. The bold words read, *Fatal Mine Accident*. A man was killed while traversing a mine shaft. He left a wife and four children. Stomach tight once again, Jesse turned the paper over. "How am I going to do this, God?"

~

TWO MONTHS LATER
CARIBOO MOUNTAIN, IDAHO

*L*orraine Durand dropped another sliver of meat into the claw-marked dirt. A sagebrush lizard bit off a portion of the jerky and raced with it across the dusty earth on the banks of Tin Cup Creek. Cariboo Mountain offered a reprieve. Here the cool air invigorated, the wild grouse picked its way along, and the creeks ran in sparkling streams. Ah, yes, a glimmer of peace...despite her nefarious reason for being here.

The other gang members were stationed away from the road but close enough to see the shipment when it came by.

In the shade of pines that grew along the stream, Beau Fox stood in the nearby creek, water up to his knees, his gun belt hanging around his thin hips and shirtsleeves rolled to his elbows.

"I got one! A gold nugget." He grinned and switched to their native language. "*Pépite d'or.*"

Lorraine raised her eyebrows in response.

Beau sloshed forward, and the men waiting by the road hurried to see the treasure. The two Baker brothers were Americans, but even if they had been French, she would still keep her distance. It was better that way. Easier. Though clad in her work clothes—canvas britches, chaps, boots, a denim shirt, and a gun belt—she knew better than to get too close. She was female and, to make matters worse, she was in charge.

Of course, Beau made his way over, smashing the lizard's jerky under his large boot when he plopped down on the log beside her. "Look here, Lorrie." He spoke French again, as he pinched a golden pea-sized nugget between forefinger and thumb.

"You are a rich man." She gulped from her canteen, then offered it to him. Sure, it was a mite familiar, but in the wild, some notions of politeness were left alone. One always shared their food and drink with their fellows.

"Nothing compared to what's gonna be coming around that there bend any time now." One of the brothers pointed to the curve in the nearby dirt road.

Lorraine wiped sweat from her eyes, her hands shaking.

"You are nervous." Beau hunched his shoulders, not looking a bit uneasy himself.

"Yes, if someone gets hurt..." All she could do was shake her head.

"That is what you are here for." He nudged her, and she swayed to the side, then came back to center.

"I don't want him to think he can just call me in on a job. This is not the life for me. I refused to come west years ago for that very reason. If it weren't for the people in New Caledonia—"

"You don't have to worry. I won't let anything happen to you." He gave her a serious nod.

Lorraine made sure not to meet his gaze too long. Though sometimes Beau focused on her with care that could be more, she knew better than to compromise their friendship. They had seen too much war together, too much suffering. More importantly, he'd chosen the life of a marauder. That wasn't for her. She just needed to finish this job and head back East.

The lizard she'd been entertaining before Beau joined her crept from between two rocks, his scales casting a pattern of browns and tans. The pounding of a horse's hooves silenced the company. The brothers, a pair nearly identical with cowhide vests and double pistol belts, withdrew farther into the trees.

Lorraine tossed her jerky toward her four-legged visitor and tucked her hair up into her tan Stetson. The last of their gang,

Pierre Martin, rode through the trees. He was a slender Frenchman with a mean squint, whom Loraine had never liked, but her boss said he had to be there, so she made sure he put her in charge.

"It's on its way." He swung down off his horse, flashing large square teeth and clutching his gun.

"No killing." She spoke to all the men, narrowing her eyes on those new to their company. "We are not here to murder. If you are fast enough and smart enough, you don't need to kill."

Beau interpreted for the newcomers as he checked the straps of his saddle.

Annoyance flickered in Pierre's face. "There was trouble with the wagon. At least that's what I heard at the camp. Should come around that bend any minute."

"Good. Emil wants us back by May twenty-first." At the thought of the date, a cold shiver passed through Lorraine. The shadows of her past crept into her mind, but she forced them away. She could not risk distraction at this moment.

Lorraine swung onto her horse. "In position?"

Already, the brothers had slingshots ready. Beau had the extra horses by the reins, and Lorraine patted her own mount's neck. Silvia was tense, the muscles beneath her black coat rippling, as though she, too, was excited for the race ahead.

"No killing." She aimed the direction of her glare at Pierre, who chuckled.

"A saintly bandit? You know, when you get to the pearly gates, they're still not going to let you in."

The rumble of iron wheels on the dirt road sounded. Beau hunched down, and Pierre inspected his nails while the Americans positioned themselves, one behind a boulder and the other around a large pine.

The horses came up the road at a swift clip, probably to recover lost time. The driver held four sets of reins, and at his side, a tall young man of about twenty gripped a rifle. The wagon was weighted down, and though she couldn't see the cargo, there were two more men with sawed-off shotguns riding rear guard.

Pierre whistled low. "Three guards and the driver. You better hope them boys are good shots." He drew his sidearm. "Don't worry. I'll be ready."

She shook her head. At least she didn't have to see him after this job.

The transport rolled by with a racket of rumbling wood and horses' hooves. A rock flew through the air, then another, dropping one rear guard, followed by the next. Neither one landed badly, so both men should recover.

Lorraine pressed her heels into Silvia's sides, and the horse bounded forward. The ground rushed beneath her, the scene ahead blurred by clouds of dust. The driver and last remaining guard sat on the seat, not noticing their incapacitated comrades. The rocks that flew next missed, hitting the wagon with a loud thump. So much for the Baker brothers being so handy with their slings as promised. Should she pull off? No, if she did, Pierre might put his pistol to use.

Lorraine rode closer, and her mount—less burdened than the team—caught up quickly. She stabilized her feet on the seat of the saddle, as she often did as part of her equestrian act for the circus, then leapt into the back of the wagon.

The guard whirled, bringing his weapon with him as Lorraine drew her Colt revolver. An explosion of gunpowder from the man's weapon racked her ears. She looked down expecting to see blood, but he'd fired past her. She brought the butt of her weapon down on his head, knocking him senseless. Lorraine dragged him back over the seat, only to receive a fist to the gut. The driver held the reins with one hand and swung wildly with the other.

She cracked him over the head and grasped for the reins before they could slip away. His dead weight shifted toward the edge of the wagon, the wheel below a blur of spinning iron. Pulling hard, Lorraine flipped him into the wagon bed and climbed into the seat. Feet staked apart, she jerked on the reins, shouting for the team to slow.

Finally, the team stopped, huffing and grumbling as though she had targeted them and not their masters. Dust floated around her. Beau rode up, yipping and laughing. Next, the brothers arrived and went straight for the gold.

Lorraine hooked the reins around the holder and set the brake. She went to the horses, calming the poor beasts with her voice and rubbing down their backs. Silvia came trotting up, whinnying at Lorraine as though she were celebrating.

Pierre, an expert at knots and binding of ropes, secured the driver first. "Good work, Lorraine. I checked the two that fell. Out cold."

"Alive?"

"Yes, blast it. Oh, but look." He rolled the young guard onto his back. "This one is dead."

"*Non!*" She jerked her head around, though Pierre laughed. He was always baiting her.

"You are one dangerous female. Look at all the blood." He hefted the man aside to reach the gold.

The front guard lay at an odd angle. She checked his pulse. Fast but steady. A paste of sweat and blood matted the hair to his temples. The cut was not deep. Still, the red turned her stomach. He looked to be in his twenties like her, tall and strong, yet somehow he seemed younger. The poor fool probably didn't know what troubles life could bring him.

The Baker brothers laughed and grunted as they transferred bags of gold into saddlebags.

Squatting in the bed, Pierre withdrew a bag and unsheathed his knife.

"We do not have time for that." Lorraine strode to the tailgate.

"What, a woman who does not enjoy riches?" Pierre laughed, threads shredding against his blade.

Sweat pouring down the side of her scalp, Lorraine removed her hat for a moment. Her associate drew out a measure of gold. It glittered in the breeze, sweeping toward her. The flecks coated her skin like the sheen of satin. Beautiful, yes, but far more importantly, funds that would be spent on those who, unlike her, had not been so fortunate to escape to America.

"What is this?" One of the Baker brothers hefted a crate but swore at its contents. He sounded out the English words on a mahogany box. "American...Opti-cal Compact View Camera.'" He looked up, toothless and bright-eyed. "What's a camera doing here?"

After shoving in the last of the bags that would fit, Lorraine buckled her saddlebags while the men loaded up the extra horses she and Beau would take when the gang split up. "There is still so much gold left. We should have brought a wagon." She frowned at Pierre, who had been in contact with someone associated with the mine.

He shrugged and rolled the driver over to loot his pockets.

"Pierre, think of how much good could be done, the people..."

He shot her a glare, as though warning her. Revealing too much in front of the Bakers was unwise. Except they could not understand French. At least she assumed so. Still, she frowned at Pierre. "Did you know there would be so much?"

"No. If it was up to me, we'd be taking the lot."

Imbecile. With funds like this, Emil could fund a rescue or ransom those imprisoned. Didn't Pierre care about their cause?

When one of the men nearly fell under the weight of the gold, Pierre laughed. Nothing of what had happened in Paris seemed to affect him, even though he had kin there during the

Bloody Week. How could he just go on with his life? Selfish man.

At last the gold was loaded, and Lorraine and Beau went in the opposite direction of the men, heading toward a neighboring mine. The gold would be shipped out as though it was dug there, not in the Alexander mine.

She glanced back, a strange prickling at her neck, only to see Pierre and the brothers still near the wagon. One man unhitched a horse while another lifted the handsome young guard. Pierre was motioning back toward the fallen guards down the road. What were they up to?

CHAPTER 2

*J*esse's bones were cement, head pounding like the striking of a hammer on an anvil. Dust filled his nose, and water trickled far off. He struggled to the surface of consciousness, awareness that all was not well pricking the back of his neck. Ropes cut into his wrists, bending them in front of him.

A woman's voice railed in French, and a man answered as vehemently.

He squinted his eyes, blurry forms taking shape in a grove of trees with campfire ablaze. There stood two people, their bodies tense as though about to fight.

Jesse's headache intensified. Memories thundered back to him like a stampede of bison. He'd been riding shotgun when he'd felt more than seen someone behind him. All he glimpsed was a tan Stetson. There had been no time to aim. With his finger already on the trigger, he pulled a second before the shot sounded and everything went black.

He'd been jumped and was now trussed up like a Thanksgiving roast. All that gold from Pa's mine had been taken. Dirty thieves. They probably wanted to ransom him too. Not if he could help it. He'd find a way to get loose. The bonds at his ankles and wrists held when he tested them, his breath coming faster. He needed to listen and figure out what was going on.

The French he'd learned as a boy sounded clearer now. He'd not heard it spoken in two years, since Maman died. Now a language he'd only ever heard spoken in love was used in an argument. Jesse lowered his eyelids, not wanting anyone to notice he was conscious.

"Taking the kid was part of the plan. You just weren't supposed to know about it." The taller of the two people wore a red bandanna. He jabbed a finger at the shorter one who spoke with a woman's voice.

"I don't believe it. You got greedy and took this man when you found out he is the owner's son."

"Think what you wish. You shouldn't even be here. I only need two men for this job—and that's the Baker brothers. You and Beau can go to Salt Lake and celebrate your bloody holiday."

All fell quiet, except for the crackle of the fire and nicker of horses. Jesse scanned the area, glimpsing three other men, one very near, forcing him to close his eyes.

The woman spoke measured words. "Very well. If you only need two, it will be Beau and me." Her voice changed, as though she turned her head. "You two men may go. Your services are not needed. Beau, tell them in English."

"You are not running this show!" the man shouted.

"I am—" There was a rustle, then all fell quiet.

A second man spoke, his voice tight. "Pierre. Lorraine. We've made a nice camp here and don't need any gunplay."

Gunplay? Jesse cracked an eyelid to find the woman in the pants with a pistol aimed at the man—presumably, Pierre.

The Frenchman curled his fingers around his weapon, which still remained in its holster. He must have gone for his gun, but the woman beat him to the draw.

"I'm in charge." Voice as cold as steel, Lorraine thumbed back the hammer, setting the gears to clicking. "I am not letting this man"—she pointed to Jesse, to which he closed his eyes—"out of my sight until I speak with Emil."

"Fine." Pierre plopped down on a log to poke the fire. "But he'll just tell you what I did, and then you'll prove what a fool-hardy, empty-headed female you are." He chuckled and straightened out his legs, crossing them at the ankles. "I'll take last watch."

"Surprising, that." Lorraine holstered her weapon, then stepped to the fire. There she checked a kettle and uncorked a bottle.

She was slender and moved with a swift confidence. A litheness her counterparts did not possess—even the wiry, thin-lipped Pierre.

The gang was obviously not united. Now, how to escape them? He was severely outnumbered and wounded. There were four men total. Pierre, the one of average height who fought with the woman. A tall fella by the horses. Lorraine had called him Beau. The two stalky, unwashed, balding men who looked like kin. The woman was his best bet. She was against his capture and obviously weaker, at least of body, despite her quick draw and wit. Who ever heard of a woman bandit? Of course, this was Idaho Territory—the Wild West.

Lorraine made her way around the fire, and Jesse quickly closed his eyes. Her boots scuffed the dirt near his head.

The fire crackled and an owl hooted amid the softly swaying branches above, playing their gentle melody that mocked his current predicament.

Why was she just standing there? He measured his breath, forcing calm. If she knew he was alert, she might suspect he had heard the argument.

"Are you awake?" She still spoke in French, her voice so soft, it sent a painful jab through him.

Maman had sounded like that.

She nudged his arm and this time sounded closer, as though having knelt down. "Monsieur, I need to tend your head wound. It will hurt."

He glared, only to lose his breath. Deep, dark eyes peered at him from within the shadow of a tan Stetson.

"Do you understand my language?" She reached for a cloth.

Jesse dodged her, only to find himself stuck between a saddle blanket on the ground and a log at his back.

She raised one midnight-black eyebrow, still speaking in French. "Do not be stubborn. Would you prefer infection?"

"I'd prefer to not be kidnapped!" He replied in the language his mother had always spoken with such tenderness.

She darted her gaze away, cheeks darker, though the men around the fire snickered. "Don't be a fool. You are already hurt, and fighting will only cause you more pain."

A tall man hunched beside the woman—Beau, the one who had tended the horses and tried to defuse tension between Lorraine and Pierre. Face lightly bearded and nose slightly bent, he scowled. "No one is untying you, so leave the lady alone."

"Lady? I thought you were all just outlaws. It's going to get plenty awkward around here if she's a lady because I need to relieve myself."

Beau cocked an eyebrow. "Let's hope you're better at controlling your body than you are at guarding gold."

Jesse flexed his shoulders, pulling against the ropes. If he wasn't tied up, he'd knock the smirk off the man's face.

"Shouldn't you take care of your needs before I tend your wound?" Lorraine fussed with the cloth.

His cheeks heated further. Darn it, he was embarrassed to speak so frankly in the presence of a woman. But she was a bandit.

"I think he can wait." Beau chuckled and, after giving the woman an encouraging nudge, went to another spot by the fire.

Back molars aching, Jesse looked up toward the tree limbs, aglow with firelight. A crimp in his neck mocked his pride, as did the pressing in his bladder.

Something touched his head, then burning broke across his scalp. He shifted his focus to the woman who withdrew a cloth from his forehead.

"The wound must be cleaned." She spilled more alcohol onto the cloth. When she reached for him again, he held still. After all, he needed the treatment. It burned like fire.

He forced his lips to stay closed against a groan.

"The wound is not so deep it needs sewing. This swelling is very good. Better to swell out than inward. Come, sit up so I can bandage your head." She grabbed his tied, booted feet and pulled them forward.

Jesse struggled to sit, once more assisted by Lorraine when she gave him a great heave. She dropped down beside him, perching comfortably on one booted foot. Though her pants were baggy, when she bent one leg at the knee, the fabric hugged the contours of her shapely calf. He looked away, resisting the urge to admire her. What was wrong with him? He should be planning his escape. This woman was his enemy and had robbed his father's mine. This was why women should not wear pants. How was a man supposed to even think straight with such a distraction?

"Bend your head down so I can reach." She drew nearer, the bandages ready, and Jesse found himself obeying her.

Hating that he felt like a schoolboy, he frowned at her. Every time she wound the cloths around his head, the air between them warmed. She was even more beautiful than he first realized, her features feminine and delicate but not childish like Aubrey's. Lorraine set her mouth in a rigid frown, the ends pulled down yet not detracting from the notable pout of her lips.

Jesse shut her out until she finished.

Suddenly, the woman moved away. "Beau, the man says he needs to water a tree."

Jesse's cheeks burned. Aubrey would never say anything so coarse.

Oh no...Aubrey. She would be so worried when she learned he was kidnapped. Pa would put off returning home since Jesse was missing. In the last two months since he'd been at the Cariboo Mountain mine, Aubrey had not written to him, but their aunt had. There'd been some change, but for the worse. Aubrey had become more withdrawn and secretive, as he knew she would. He was supposed to get her a photo of the lake, bring her back to who she was, but instead, he was tied up and at the mercy of a pistol-toting female.

Lorraine arranged the items she'd used to treat him beside a large wooden box with a mahogany side. Aubrey's camera! The gang had taken it from the wagon. But where had they stored all the gold? Aside from their supplies, the camera was the only stolen item he could see.

The tall man who liked horses came over, bending over Jesse as though he was a child. "Hey, kid, let's go."

Once Beau had untied his ankles, he tied a rope to Jesse's belt loop and gave it a quick yank before announcing it would hold. He led Jesse into the trees where cool air and darkness lent to the calm. No sooner had Jesse finished what he meant to do than footfalls drew near.

Lorraine whispered something to Beau, her voice sharp and conspiratorial. "You know he won't, though. He's too selfish and won't want to wake up."

"Them Baker brothers are lazy too. Sleep as sound as bears in winter too."

"You take first watch. I'll take second. Don't even bother waking Pierre."

So the woman would take second watch? Jesse wrestled his suspenders into place as best he could while trussed up. He'd have to figure out some way to overpower her, escape during her shift. The gold shipment had left the camp late that day, so this retched gang of outlaws couldn't have gotten far in the dark. The sooner he escaped, the better.

≈

A bloodcurdling scream rang from Lorraine's dream, as real as the day it pierced her ears. Waking in a cold sweat, she captured the noise inside where she always kept it. The forest in Idaho closed around her for an instant, then she slipped back into memory. Amid the black of slumber quaked the thunder of feet. The rumble of horses' hooves. Then the executioners' volleys. The thumping of bodies hitting the ground.

Someone drew near. Lorraine opened her eyes. A large man leaned over her, silhouetted against a moonlit sky and pine branches. She slapped at him, only to find her arm gently pushed away.

"Calm, Lorrie. It is only me."

"Oh, Beau." She fell back against the saddle she used for her pillow, shivering.

"It's your watch." Beau stifled a yawn, then stepped over her to go to his spot.

Limbs shaky and skin damp, Lorraine made her way past the smoldering campfire. The prisoner sat up, startling her to a stop. It was as though he'd been waiting for her.

His low voice rumbled in the darkness. "I need a break."

Was he playing her false? Likely. She continued on her way.

"Please?"

His plea stopped her, the nightmare still clinging to her and reminding her of life's fragility. How fortunate she was to be here, alive. Fortunate? Could one claim such when they were forever lost? Separated from their home?

"Are you going to help me?" He raised his voice this time, though the men slept on.

Lorraine drew near him, crossing her arms. "You could have relieved yourself during Beau's watch, but you waited until mine began. You think because I am female, that you will overpower me."

He stiffened, his face exposed by moonlight. "If you don't feel comfortable, wake up your friend."

But Beau had just gone to rest. If Pierre and the Bakers woke up and saw, they would think her weak. "There is no need." Lorraine drew her Colt, the solid handle a comfort in her palm. She twirled it, took aim at the log just behind his head, then holstered it. "Just remember this—I may be the smallest, but I am the fastest."

"And the meanest. Likely, the best aim and the smartest too. All the more reason to not ask you for assistance." He held her gaze, eyes veiled beneath thick lashes. "That, and the fact that you are a lady."

Maybe he had not been waiting on her. No. She could not afford to hope for such a thing, thereby making herself vulnerable to an attack. Still, Lorraine untied the bounds at his ankles, leaving one yet secure so she could knock him over with a yank. Her prisoner rose slowly.

Prisoner. She hated being party to something so evil, but she couldn't take on Pierre and the Baker brothers, forcing Beau to choose a side. All he had was the gang, and after losing everything in France, he needed the French community Emil provided. Pierre was lying about the kidnapping being sanctioned by their boss. He had to be.

He groaned and stretched his arms. "Will you loosen my wrists?"

She yanked the rope tied to his ankle, nearly toppling him to the ground.

He glowered at her, so tall she had to crane her head back.

Lorraine motioned him toward a stand of trees. Pine needles rustled beneath their feet until she drew him to a halt. "On the tree."

"You're going to watch?" Disbelief, anger, and disgust echoed through his voice.

Lorraine motioned again, yet moved as far as the rope allowed when the rustle of fabric told her he was readying himself. Cheeks hot, she looked away. She should have awakened Beau. But no. After Pierre's comments the night before, she'd felt the need to prove herself.

When the prisoner was finished, he walked back, dry pine needles crunching beneath his boots. She couldn't hold his gaze, though he stopped too near for comfort. "Well, at least you have some decency."

That Maman had raised her with, despite the less than glorious life they'd lived traveling from town to town performing.

She tugged the rope, but he staked his feet in place.

"Can't we just wait here a little while?" He angled his face up.

Moonlight traced the bridge of his nose, a little thick but not in a way that made him less attractive. Indeed, he was all manly bulk in the right places with a firm jaw and mouth, and clever eyes. She'd not be taken for a fool, though. He was easily embarrassed—proof of his innocence—but he was not gullible. Yet with his gaze on the heavens, he seemed harmless, like a statue.

"I haven't taken the time to look at the stars in ages." He sounded weary, a feeling she knew all too well.

She hugged herself to chase away the chill, shadows from her dreams still clawing at her back. "Why look at all? They never change."

He snapped his gaze around, amazement written in his features. "They change all the time." A blaze of silver streaked by and fizzled out just overhead as though to prove her wrong. "Look at that. Do you want the wish?"

Lorraine shook her head. She'd give him his stars, nothing more.

He stared for a while, his wide chest heaving. Moonlight set the white of his plaid shirt bright, the fabric stretching between his shoulders. He was strong, intelligent, and wealthy. What could he even want?

"What did you wish for?" she asked.

"To be free. What else?"

If only making wishes brought such things.

"Why did you take me?"

Wishing on stars wouldn't give him freedom or answers, and neither would she.

"You were a greater number, weren't you? The gang split up, right? I didn't see a wagon. Some men took the gold, and you and this bunch took me?"

She gave him her gaze, for pity more than anything. The poor man would see himself beaten senseless and flung over a horse before he saw freedom. Such was the ruthlessness of this gang. "You wish to make sense of what you do not control. There is no control, American. It is an illusion as is freedom. You will find neither here." As she had not, though his chances might be better than hers.

He scoffed. For a long moment, all was quiet except for the hooting of an owl and the scurry of a raccoon's clawed feet when the creature passed them without a glance.

"Why did you take me?" Voice quieter now, he spoke without the usual demands.

If only she could answer that question.

He rocked on his heels. "My mother was French."

Ah, so that was how he knew her language.

"I thought I was dreaming when I heard you speak. It is such a beautiful language."

That brought her the quiver of a smile.

"Your French is perfect, but you don't know English. Why are you in America?"

"Why does a learned man of your youth ride shotgun on a gold shipment?"

He sighed and looked away, shrugging. "I wanted adventure."

She stiffened, something in his manner offsetting. "You lie."

He swung back around. "Why be truthful with a bandit? Any information could be used to my disadvantage. I could tell you my name was Ulysses S. Grant and it wouldn't matter."

She scoffed. "You are far too young and handsome for even a blind man to believe that."

He cocked his head, then laughed. The sound was strained but true.

Who was this man, and why did Pierre think Emil would want him? Could it have something to do with her business with Emil? Blood suddenly cold, she tightened her fists. "Does your father ship to faraway lands? Australia, perhaps?" She pressed her teeth together, hope a taut thread ready to break.

"No."

"Do you have any connection with France?"

"Nope. Just that my maman came from there and refused to speak English in our home. She said it was a coarse language."

Lorraine raised her chin. "Compared to French, all are."

"No humility there."

"I see no reason for any."

He shook his head, an unreadable expression in place.

Might he share his laughter again? Moonlight caressing his stubbly jaw, he turned, arms crossed. "What is your name?"

Holding eye contact for fear he might try to overpower her, she answered. "Lorraine. Yours?"

"Jesse. Why are you here, Lorraine?"

Here in America? At the camp after the robbery? Or standing before him in the wilderness instead of at her post?

"You are educated, even if you try to be crude."

She sniffed. "Such bold statements for one with a recent head wound. How do you know I am educated? You barely know my language."

"Let me guess. You had a hard life, but there was someone —a benefactor, godfather, or mentor of some kind—who saw to your education."

Emil, who had come to the camps on the outskirts of Paris to take her away from her people to *Château d'Écouen*. Always, she tried to escape. But the emperor's school had forced education upon her despite her mother's heritage. Of course, Château d'Écouen had not been the prison she believed it to be. No, there had been a worse fate awaiting her once she completed her studies. Once the Germans invaded.

The memories came flooding back, including Maman's lifeless gaze and pale face. Soldiers had dragged Lorraine away, their grips like iron clamps. Regardless of the pain, she'd cried for Maman. She had fought for freedom, jabbing, kicking, biting, and slapping.

A force hit her from the side, her feet knocked out from under her.

She curled her back and rolled with momentum. Strong arms brushed around her, hands clawing as they sought to take hold. She slipped free. Feet in the dirt, Lorraine drew her Colt and pulled back the hammer.

Jesse—not a soldier—froze on his knees before her, his powerful shoulders trembling and his eyes alight with disbelief.

She pressed her finger against the trigger, but before she could pull it back, someone tackled Jesse to the ground. He landed in an unconscious heap.

Beau knelt nearly on top of Jesse and drew back the fist he'd just used to knock their prisoner out. "Lorraine?" He eased the tip of the revolver up, his voice soft. "I thought you wanted to protect this man?"

Shaking, she slipped her fingers from cool steel. "He tried to hurt me."

"Of course he did. If you wished to avoid such, you should have woken me up."

She should have, but then she'd felt compassion for Jesse. He'd made her feel normal for a moment. "I was a fool, I know. But what would you have me do?"

"I hope this is truly your only job. This life, Lorrie—it will turn you into something your maman would be ashamed of."

"He attacked me. Pierre can take him wherever he likes. I care not."

He dragged Jesse back to camp, leaving Lorraine to settle into her place of lookout. Yet Beau's words still haunted. If he hadn't stepped in when he did, the forest floor would be wet with blood. Jesse had attacked her when her thoughts were dark with memories. She hadn't been ready. Had lost her grip on what was real. She wasn't safe around anyone. Had gone too far from the woman Maman and even the nuns raised her to be.

Lorraine pressed the back of her head against the rough bark of a pine. "Have I lost myself, God?" The question remained unanswered, though Lorraine's thoughts raced through what had occurred with Jesse until sleep settled them to rest.

When the sun arose, Lorraine found that while she'd succumbed to weariness, the Baker brothers—the Americans —had run off, taking with them a supply of goods. And the camera, of all things. Since they had been Pierre's guide through the Idaho Territory, he asked Beau to get them to the nearest railroad. Blessedly, Beau's only condition was that Lorraine remain as well. And so, she found herself Jesse's guardian, after all.

CHAPTER 3

*H*eat ebbed as shadows lengthened, the noon hours having slipped away to welcome evening. Lorraine rode down a rocky slope to an open plain spotted with junipers and sage. After two days on the trail—and that was just since the robbery—she was ready for a cool bath, soft petticoats, and the support of a boned corset instead of the cotton one she currently wore. Unfortunately, the three-day ride to the nearest railroad would not allow for such feminine finery. Three days. Still, plenty of time to make it to Salt Lake by the twenty-first.

"We'll have to camp here." Beau narrowed his gaze on the settlement of Soda Springs cropping up like part of the land here in the wild.

Pierre rode beside a stern-faced Jesse, whose bruising was dark as ever, though the man seemed no more distressed than any of the others who had ridden the two days from Cariboo.

The morning the Baker brothers ran off, Pierre had declared he was in charge because Emil had trusted him, not Lorraine, with the prisoner. She had pressed him further for information on Jesse but had received little. How would she deal with a power struggle she didn't even want? She hadn't asked to be put in charge of raiders. She was better suited for the circus, but for this job, her combined skills in riding and shooting, and maybe her sheer cunning in general, had made her the obvious choice. This wasn't the life she wanted, ever. If they could just get enough money to send to her friends and neighbors still in chains...

"Trouble." Beau steered his horse to cut across at her side, and Silvia followed with nary a complaint. The mare must have sensed Lorraine's trust in Beau, for she'd not reacted so to anyone else. Perhaps the beast sensed the danger Lorraine did when three riders with the typical straw Mormon hats bore down on them, guns at the ready. The religious farmers were known to have guards patrolling their settlements in case of trouble. Not a group to be trifled with.

She pressed in her heels, Pierre's curses muffled in the pounding of horses' hooves. Jesse must have sensed his chance because he twisted his reins to the right, veering away from the group. If he escaped, he would turn them in, giving the nearest law enforcement a description of Beau, who could not afford any more attention from the law. Beau had wanted to go back to Salt Lake after they transported the gold to the appointed place, but Lorraine had convinced him to see what Pierre was up to. When the Baker brothers left, Beau was the only one familiar with the area to guide them. If he was caught and turned over now...

Lorraine shifted her reins and urged Silvia to the left, placing Jesse between herself and Pierre. She knocked her mount into his. Both horses were startled. Jesse quickly regained control.

Gunshots cracked over the open field.

Hunching instinctively, Lorraine kept pace with Jesse. On the other side, Pierre reached for the reins with no success—

the clumsy louse. Riding as one with Silvia, Lorraine whistled loudly toward Jesse's horse. Sensing its confusion, she grasped the reins.

Jesse, hands still tied together, turned his body, pulling them away. More gunshots rang out. Still, he clung to the reins.

Beau steered to the right, straight for a treed area. They might outrun the farmers on their horses, but the bullets would reach across the open space, making up for the slower farm stock.

Lorraine and Pierre closed in again, each grasping a rein. Jesse shouted as he lost control of the beast. There was fury in his voice, but also something deeper. Lorraine focused on traversing the path ahead, between trees and over a stream, water spraying up on all sides.

Beau guided them with certainty. Pierre led Jesse's horse, and she fell into line behind them. The way narrowed between brush and rocks.

Jesse called for help, but Pierre swung around and aimed his revolver at him. "If you're going to bring them down on us, we might as well be done with it."

Both men glanced back at her as though looking for an ally. Lorraine hardened her features, uninterested in either of them getting her or Beau killed.

The stream slowed and settled out into marshy earth.

"Beau, where are you taking us?" Pierre complained when his horse struggled in the mud.

"Here." Beau drew to a halt beside strange rocks that formed thick, shoulder-high walls. "Lorrie, take Jesse into the terraced pools. Follow this trail here."

"She's not going off with this kid." Pierre glared at Beau, who ignored him.

Lorraine swung out of her saddle and, surprisingly, Jesse did the same.

Beau pointed down one of the rows. "Go right at the fork,

then in forty strides, there's a cave. You can hide there. Pierre and I will lead the farmers away."

"You can't leave them. He'll try to jump her again." Pierre plopped down into the water and stalked toward Jesse. "Lorraine, go with Beau."

"No." Beau took the reins from Pierre. "If they get close, they'll see she's a woman and report it. Two men passing through is one thing. Having her along makes us more conspicuous."

"Which is why she shouldn't be here." Pierre slammed his gun against the side of Jesse's head, and he dropped to his knees.

Lorraine looked away, a protest behind her lips, but Jesse had already tried to hurt her. She shouldn't even care.

With Jesse nearly unconscious, Pierre checked the ropes. His movements were swift and rough. Jesse's swollen red hands twitched but remained with the ropes cutting near his flannel sleeve cuffs.

"Hurry." Beau watched the way they'd come. "They're going to catch up. Pierre, you better gag him so he doesn't shout and give away Lorraine's position."

"No," Jesse muttered, his head nodding as blood drained down one side of his face.

Lorraine drew a bandanna from her saddlebags and quickly cinched the gag around his mouth. "Resisting is fruitless. Cooperate, and I will not hurt you." She kept her voice quiet. If her compatriots overheard, they would see her weakness.

"Here, Lorrie, take the rope in case you need to tie his feet." Beau offered a lariat from his saddle, and she swung it over one shoulder.

Pierre mounted with a threat to Lorraine and Jesse, then followed Beau, who, bless him, did not even glance back to make sure she knew what to do. Gun already drawn, she motioned Jesse between two high rock walls. He actually went without hesitation.

~

*H*ead throbbing where that Frenchman had smacked him, Jesse kept on through the terraced pools, which were mostly empty. His joints screamed as though they would come out of the sockets. Still, he walked on. In truth, he wasn't too keen on being overcome by the farmers. They had shot at them, after all, but might he fare better with them than the angry, pistol-happy French woman at his back?

"Duck down." Lorraine jabbed him in the ribs with the gun, long enough to make contact, then she drew away again, keeping her distance—most likely, so he could not judge her location and seize her. She was astute, experienced. He'd been a fool for trying to take her so soon after being captured. Not just because his headache and sore ribs had put him at a disadvantage, but also because he did not know his foe. The slippery lady had moved with incredible speed, her recovery far swifter than anything he'd imagined from a woman. He'd wasted his chance to gain her trust. That night under the stars, she'd been less guarded. Since he'd attacked her, she barely looked at him. When she did, it was with cold disinterest. She also hadn't continued her argument with Pierre regarding his kidnapping.

They came to a fork in the pools and went right. Soon, the dark hole in the rocks dropped down into the ground.

Jesse bit into the gag and steadied himself, making his way down the incline. The temperature fell quickly, cooling his warm skin. He stumbled on the rocky cave floor. If he'd been here with any other woman, and under extremely different circumstances, he would have warned Lorraine that the way was uncertain and assisted her. What was he thinking? This woman didn't need help.

A weight fell against him. Lorraine gasped and clutched his arms, pulling down on his sore joints. His ropes dug in deeper, yet he steadied himself to support her and met her gaze over his shoulder.

Just enough light slipped through the cave opening to settle on her eyes of brown scattered with gold, like the raw flecks found in Cariboo Mountain streams. Lorraine thrust herself away as though he was a spider with eight free legs instead of the bound man he was.

"Feel with your feet as you move forward, and listen for water." She urged him onward, this time with a shove.

The ground sloped down, the space ahead black as a winter solstice night. He'd rather stay near the opening. What if there was a drop-off? They might plunge to their deaths. He hunched as he walked. The last thing he needed was another blow to the head.

Lorraine used her one free hand as a guide. "You sit, and I will find the way forward. It could be dangerous."

And yet she, far smaller, would go ahead of him? He could not have that. While she might be a faster draw and better horseman than he, his experience in mines would surpass hers.

"Sit." She motioned toward the shadow-laden side of the cave.

He shook his head again.

"I said, sit." This time she pushed him, but he staked his feet on the rocky dirt floor.

Lorraine tried again, tugged on his arm. He steadied himself, resisting her easily and towering over her. She darted to his back and kicked at the backs of his knees, but Jesse shifted to face her, poised for another attack. She raised her chin to meet his gaze, clutching her holstered weapon. Was he pushing too hard and about to be shot?

"Foolish, prideful man. I will go on without you." She stalked forward two paces, then spun. "You know what I must do if you run? I will not sacrifice myself or Beau for you —American."

Any notion that she might help him far gone, he inclined his head. Regardless, if she wanted him to sit, she would have to do the same. He nodded toward the rocky edge of the cave and raised his eyebrows.

"You want me to sit?" She snickered. "That you might sooner have me on my back?"

That forced outrage through him. What kind of life had this woman lived? Had she suffered as Aubrey had?

"I will not sit this close to the opening," Lorraine said. "If they happen upon us, you will try to alert them despite the gag. I will not die for you."

There was that statement again. He needn't be reminded, though. Perhaps if he sat down, she would. Minding his head where the cave ceiling lowered, Jesse swiped away pebbles with one foot, then sat down.

Lorraine disappeared into the darkness, though she returned shortly after and stationed herself between him and the opening.

The minutes dragged by. Jesse bit down on the moist gag, his body aching after two days riding by horseback. He hung his head. In the dark of himself, he found a prayer, though it was for Aubrey and Pa, for the guards and driver in the holdup who had been hurt, and for the workers who might suffer because of the money lost. He'd been so angry with his captors that he'd not considered the others affected by this event. They were hurt all because of a bunch of selfish thieves.

His vision adjusted to the gray planes and slopes of the cave. Lorraine shivered a few feet away with her arms wrapped around her knees. She wasn't a very big package but still dangerous. Like a fox, cunning and vicious. He had to remember that.

Taking out a canteen, she unscrewed the lid, then drank

long gulps, her slender throat moving slightly with the action. She lowered it and met his gaze. He gave her a questioning look.

"The water will cost you." She thumbed the lid back on the canteen and reached for the rope Beau had given her. "I will not have you kick my brains out, then run to the farmers for help."

Again, her accusations disturbed. Though she had reason to doubt him. True, they were far away from Cariboo Mine. The farmers could take him to Soda Springs, though.

Why shouldn't he risk Lorraine's safety for the chance to escape and return to Pa and Aubrey? Doing so was right and brave, regardless of the cost to Lorraine—a thief.

Resignation tightened Lorraine's mouth as though she heard his thoughts. She set the canteen and rope aside.

He straightened his legs and grunted, begrudgingly submitting.

She stationed herself near his boots, then met his gaze. "If you seek to hurt me, I will kill you." Despite her words, there was a pleading in her eyes.

Jesse closed her out, resisting anger, feeling and not seeing the ties she made around his ankles before she moved beside him. Her arm brushed his. She worked the bandanna free.

The fabric came loose, and Jesse pressed his cracked lips together.

Lorraine traded the gag for the canteen and uncorked it. "You'll need to tip back your head."

The cold spout touched his lips. He gulped, his parched throat blessedly cool. Lorraine gave him his fill, then eased the canteen back, avoiding his gaze. She offered her profile, her delicate nose swooping down to full lips.

Jesse hardened his features. The last thing he needed was her sensing his attraction. Let all that was sane be hanged, he found her lovely. But she was a thief!

Voices called through the opening. Lorraine rose to her feet and held one finger to her lips. The voices grew louder. Her lips moved without sound, as though in a silent prayer. The mask was back. She was the outlaw. Revolver at the ready, she strode toward the entrance of the cave.

"Stop. Lorraine, you don't have to kill them." He leaned toward her, trying to force his whisper after her.

She shook her head yet kept on.

"Please? You said you'd not die for me. Don't kill because of me."

That stilled her.

What more could he say? What did this woman even care about? "Beau. He wouldn't want you to kill for him either."

She returned to him, walking slowly. "You want them here in the cave, bullets flying? Perhaps you hope they will trap me here and kill me."

Jesse recoiled, keeping his voice as soft as hers. "Why do you believe I am so vile? I do not wish harm to you or Beau. You seem...decent. For bandits."

A smirk lifted her cheeks. She glanced at the lighted way, then to her weapon before lowering herself beside him. This time she leaned her head back on a rock. The men's voices lessened, then grew by degree. Lorraine's jaw twitched. Why hadn't she put the gag back on him? What did she have planned? To shoot him if they were discovered? If so, she would be sadly disappointed. He might be tied, but as close as she was, he could shove her over and hold her down until the farmers answered his calls. But as long as she held the weapon, she was lethal. He flexed his hands and feet.

"You know, I think I dreamed this." Lorraine's finger was no longer on the trigger.

Which was good for him if he was going to overpower her. "What do you mean?" He scooted closer. "Being in a cave?"

"No. Giving up. Stop running and just fight to the end. Maybe it would be better."

"What would be better?"

She tilted her chin up, exposing a clean, slender neck. "To be done, free from all of this."

He recoiled. "You shouldn't say such things. God says when a person is born and dies. You are blessed to be in good health. Strong of mind, body, and heart."

There were the voices again. Lorraine's eyes went vague, as though she were seeing something far away. "Perhaps they will help you get home, or at least contact your pere."

Was she giving up? Should he call to the men? He licked his lips.

A raucous laugh sounded from above, so loud its owner must be looking into the cave. Lorraine startled and pointed her Colt toward the opening, lips moving in silent words.

Was she praying? "Stop." His words sounded more like a hiss. "Lorraine, don't."

"I am tired of people dying." She pulled back the hammer. "But I won't let them hurt me either."

Jesse scooted over to her. How to get her to put the gun down? What if he startled her and she fired it? He was helpless, bound as he was. Leaning his chin near her shoulder, he whispered, "We are outnumbered. Shooting at them would mean certain death."

"I..." She shook her head, breath coming fast now. "I'm tired of running. Not belonging anywhere."

"You deserve better. Put the gun down, Lorraine. Put it down, or release me and let me fight beside you."

Her eyelids lifted. Lorraine met his gaze, mere inches between their noses. There was softening again when she spoke. "You must have a very good life." She scooted away, glancing up at the cave ceiling as the voices faded. "I think they must be searching the pools. That is why their voices grow and lessen."

He nodded and looked ahead, jaw hardening. He didn't tell her that his life wasn't always good or that he'd faced his own cave. When Maman died and then Aubrey left so soon afterward, he'd closed himself into his study and fell into dark, lonely spells. No, Jesse kept his thoughts to himself. After all, he'd already shared too much with this woman. At least she wasn't about to kill someone.

CHAPTER 4

he voices faded entirely, as did the light. The temperature in the cave continued to drop, but still Jesse and Lorraine waited.

"Lorraine, we should move." He spoke English, and when she did not respond, switched to French. "Shouldn't we venture above ground for warmth, at least?"

"B-Beau said to wait." Her words came out between chattering teeth.

"He wouldn't want you becoming ill."

"He'll be back soon."

She seemed to put a lot of stock in his word, though Beau was nowhere near a leader in the outlaw trio.

Jesse rested his head on his knees, capturing warmth by drawing up his legs. His boots and pantlegs were still wet, but he did not shiver. He'd always run warm and had a significant amount of muscle compared to Lorraine.

Her teeth chattered again.

He turned his head, pointing his voice at her. "We should go above ground. It will be warmer."

The silence of pitch-black earth remained. If she were

Aubrey, he'd just hold her to warm her. Lorraine would likely shove the barrel of her gun into his throat if he did so. But she'd said she didn't want to kill anyone.

A final chatter of teeth sent Jesse into action. He looped his bound arms around Lorraine. She startled violently, careening her head into his nose.

"No! Let me go!" Her anguished cry turned his blood cold.

"Lorraine, I'm just trying to keep you from shivering to death."

She panted, warm breath fanning his jaw. She carefully touched his cheek, as though fearing his skin might scald her. "Who? Jess...Jesse? Where are we?"

The woman didn't know where she was? That was concerning, to say the least. "We are in a cave, hiding, remember? You were going to fight those men alone."

"And you stopped me. Why?"

"I did not want you to get hurt. You seemed—well, hopeless." He sighed deeply. "Lorraine, why is it so hard for you to believe that I do not wish you harm?"

"What are you doing now?" She didn't seem to have even heard his question.

Jesse cupped a hand around her, despite ropes that burned with his movements. "You were cold."

"Oh." She was very still, not even moving with breath. "You're not going to hurt me?"

Something in her voice stung his insides, and he desperately wanted to promise her safety. Instead, he shrugged. "Not much reason to, now, is there? It's not as though I could go anywhere, and besides, you're cold."

She pushed against his chest.

"Stop." He resisted the urge to shake her. "Lorraine, if you had been a man that night in the forest, I would have incapacitated you. I was afraid of hurting you. I..." He sighed long. "I couldn't grab a hold of you or bring myself to twist your arm because doing so would cause you pain. Even now, I could take you."

"Perhaps, but what keeps you from hurting me?"

"My pa raised me to treat women with respect. To cherish them, and a woman close to me was hurt. It pains me, just thinking about her." Aubrey, in all her hopeful youth. He might have offended her and others by speaking up, but at least she may have been safe.

"I'm sorry someone you love was hurt." Lorraine shrugged her shoulders as though to move away again.

Jesse spoke near her ear. "I promise, for her sake, not to harm you or try to escape while we are in the cave."

She stayed rigid, then slowly lowered her head to his collarbone. "I'm sure Beau will be back soon."

"You trust him."

"He is my friend." No four words ever sounded so clearly.

Friendship with Lorraine must be a precious thing. Something not often found nor easily gained.

The minutes stretched, and Jesse's aching back protested. He shifted, startling the criminal in his arms, but she didn't reach for her gun or claw at him again. She was very still. He couldn't imagine the thoughts running through her head in light of the impropriety of their position. A lesser woman, a wanton woman, might use their proximity to her advantage, but not Lorraine. All he felt from her was disquiet and fear, with occasional moments of rest.

What was this woman's story? Why did she seem to fade between ruthlessness and hopelessness so often? Had God allowed Jesse to be captured to show her compassion? No, that wasn't possible. God wouldn't cause something so wrong as a kidnapping to happen to work His good will. The kidnapping was sin and God was good.

Jesse sighed, weary of trying to find a way to escape, and rested his chin on Lorraine's head.

She held her breath, clasping one fist, but didn't struggle. All was still and quiet, except for Lorraine's moments where she dozed, then would awaken scared and confused. They went through the conversation again, that he'd not hurt her and they were in a dire situation together. At last, a lantern came into view.

Lorraine startled, then slipped away from him, uttering one word as she gained her feet. "Beau?"

Pierre popped his head into the hole. "I didn't think you two would actually be here. Come on up before you freeze, Lorraine."

Shadows settled a ghostliness about her. The woman was not well, but who could blame her? She had faced death in that cave.

Pierre actually helped her up before he climbed down to untie Jesse's ankles. He yanked hard, nearly knocking Jesse over. Jesse used an elbow to catch himself on the case wall, slamming it into the rocks. Pain radiated up his arm.

With Lorraine out of sight and Pierre yanking the ropes still binding his wrists, Jesse fumed. He should have tried to escape. He'd had Lorraine at his mercy. Overpowering her didn't mean hurting her. He would have left her there for Beau to find, but no. He'd been more concerned about her well-being, as though he'd forgotten the other men were coming back.

Jesse's ascent from the cave was far from graceful. He tripped and stumbled into Pierre, nearly knocking the man over. Pierre swore but cut the ropes about Jesse's wrists.

Lorraine stumbled up ahead, feeling her way among the trees. Moonlight sliced between the branches overhead and danced on the water. There was a splashing, then Beau came striding up through a shallow pool. "Lorrie, what's wrong? Did something happen?"

She responded so quietly, Jesse couldn't catch her words, but Beau promptly led her forward. They seemed close.

Friends, as Lorraine had explained. If he didn't know any better, he'd say they were family.

Beau hugged her, and she leaned into him.

Pierre's sour expression intensified at the sight of the other Frenchman. "Beau, I told you to wait with the horses. If they run off, we'll be on foot. You foolish gypsy"

Lorrain turned suddenly, lunging at Pierre, but Beau took her around the waist and turned her back around, speaking calmingly to her.

Pierre scoffed, then spoke in fairly clear English. "I have always wondered about those two."

Jesse didn't bite, though a nervousness stirred in his gut.

"Beau won't go anywhere without Lorraine when she's in town. He even works as a hired hand at that circus of hers sometimes."

"Circus?"

"*Oui*, The Sells Brothers Circus. Lorraine has worked for them for years. Every now and then, Beau gets it in his head that he needs to live a better life, and he goes to tending elephants. Must be their Roma blood."

"Roma?" Jesse kept on, stumbling on the rocky soil, though this pool was dried up.

"Roma people. They are gypsies, both of them. They grew up together. Thick as thieves, you know? One time, our boss assigned Beau a dangerous job. Before he left, Lorraine had a meeting with our boss, and a different man was sent. She's either a really good talker or good at something else." Pierre snickered, and Jesse bit down on his back teeth.

The man was a fool. Or, at least, Jesse hoped he was. After all, he knew little about Lorraine.

He caught a movement in the trees where a group of horses waited. Pierre pushed Jesse toward his mount, still complaining. Beau didn't seem to notice, his gaze following Lorraine when she took a sip from his canteen.

An expression of delight sounded from her, then Beau chuckled. He turned to Jesse. "I got one for you, too, Jess."

Trying not to bristle at being given a nickname under such circumstances, he accepted the canteen and took a drink. His mouth filled with bubbles. Oh...that was right. They were near Soda Springs. The water here was carbonated, like one might get from a barber shop. Aubrey had loved Soda Springs. He should be with Aubrey, not here with Lorraine.

Jesse grinned at Beau. "Thanks. Better than the stuff they sell in barber shops."

The Frenchman smiled, though the expression faded when Pierre neared Lorraine, offering to assist her into the saddle.

"Where we headed now?" Jesse asked Beau.

The man headed back toward Lorraine, yet answered over one shoulder. "Salt Lake."

The hair on Jesse's neck stood up at the mere mention. His last trip there had tested his own salt. He'd never describe himself as a desperado, like Lorraine, but he'd been desperate and not exactly abiding by the law. Aubrey had needed him, though, and he'd not been willing to fail his sister. No matter the cost.

Memories of her listless gaze flooded him, a promise not to fail her again swelling inside him. He had to return to her before it was too late!

～

Three days had passed since the robbery. The ride had been even harder once they passed Soda Springs, not stopping at the settlement after the run-in with the protective farmers. Lorraine reined in near a spring, the others in her company doing the same.

Water ran through the flatland here. Hills checkered with scruffy grass and rock stretched in the distance. A small town settled into the natural landscape, and a train track ran in a straight line through the settlement.

Jesse dismounted beside her, his presence like a fresh spring wind off the Sein. She'd not met his gaze since they emerged from the cave—that secret place where she'd trusted a man she did not know to protect her and felt the gentle thrill of attraction. It could not have come at a worse time.

Jesse knelt, pushing his hands into the clear stream to scoop water, his skin terribly red and swollen. Most of the water poured out, and he was left slurping.

The back of her throat tightened, and she stared in the opposite direction. Her hands had been bound like that, to the point that they turned blue. It had only been the mercy of a guard that spared her, though he'd cursed her as a petroleuse once he'd sawed through her bindings. Her fingers tingled as they had that day. Lorraine flexed them. The sensation was not real, though at times, the memories were so vivid she remained trapped in them until they passed or she fell asleep.

Lorraine drew a knife from her belt and knelt beside him. Pierre shouted a complaint, but she severed the cords, then stalked away. It made her nauseous to see Jesse suffer as she and her loved ones had. Why was she going along with this? He was a good man. Just remembering his arms around her in the cave stilled her midstride. She felt hot and even more sick, though she tried to shake the feeling away. He could have crushed her, yet he had held her tenderly. Not sacrificing her life for his freedom.

They needed to get to Salt Lake City so Emil could straighten out this mess.

Lorraine returned to her company. The men stooped to fill canteens, and the horses drank. "This is where we split up. Boarding together will be too conspicuous. Beau, you stay with Jesse. Pierre, go ahead as lookout. Find a way to sneak them aboard the train unseen."

Neither of the men contested her order, and when each went their separate ways for nature's call, Jesse turned his blue gaze on her. "What town is this?"

Barely holding eye contact due to the fluttering in her middle, she shrugged one shoulder. "Franklin, on the Utah and Idaho border."

His eyebrows jumped, and he narrowed his gaze. "Where are you taking me, Lorraine?"

She stooped to fill her canteen in the stream and twisted the cap into place.

"Do you always ignore others when they pose questions you don't like? And here I thought you a brave bandit."

"I have no answers for you, Jesse." She raised to her full height, hands on her hips, the canteen dangling by a strap from one arm. "My boss wants to see you. That's all I need to know."

"I thought you didn't believe Pierre?"

"I don't, but he will not let you go until we've spoken with our boss. When we do, he'll be proved wrong."

"Or he'll shoot you before we get there."

"Beau won't allow that to happen, and neither will I."

Jesse scoffed. "So you hope. This boss of yours? You do whatever he says, regardless of who gets hurt?"

Lorraine strapped the canteen over one shoulder, taking in a deep breath to frame an argument she did not feel. "I do what needs to be done, because that is right."

He reeled back, then barked a laugh. "You robbed my father's business, stealing from hardworking miners. Some have families back East. They are saving to move here. And you kidnapped me. You call that right?"

"You can't understand, which is why this argument is fruitless." She strode to her mare to secure her gear, her cheeks growing ever hotter.

Jesse followed her and stopped beside her mare, where he

flexed his hands. "Fine. If you can convince me, I won't try to escape anymore."

Beau's and Pierre's voices tossed on the wind, each of them striding from a different direction yet headed toward the stream. If she did not answer, they would soon be interrupted.

Lorraine faced Jesse, though the nearness of him caused something inside her to shrink. "You talk about the miners, those who need the money. Well, I have people who suffer far more than these men who have the freedom, the privilege to scratch a living out of the gold fields. Selfish American—"

"Everyone has a right to life and liberty. To pursue happiness and success. You have stolen the fruits of others' labor."

"Yes, labor for which they are paid. They will earn more money because of American freedom. Unlike my people." A trembling broke out inside her. She'd not delved into these feelings for so long because it always rattled her. The anger, fear, and utter helplessness. She strode away from Jesse's imposing stance, speaking over one shoulder. "You know nothing of hardship, of war."

"Where are your people? Don't tell me you gifted them with the gold you stole. A regular Robin Hood. You have no people. You are making excuses. Lying."

"I am not lying." Lorraine chucked the canteen at him, which he caught one handed. "You preach of rights when you have known nothing of my people's suffering."

"My pa fought in the Civil War."

"Again, stupid, selfish American. A conflict of your own, and you were on the winning side. You know nothing of siege. To have your home tread upon and defiled by the enemy." At last, he seemed to hear her, though doubt lingered around his eyes.

"I've heard of the turbulence in Europe. The war between France and Germany. Paris fell into German hands. Were you—"

"You two have another squabble?" Pierre strode up smirking. "It's no good, Jesse. Mademoiselle Durand never loses a fight."

Beau smacked Pierre on the arm. "You used her surname in front of him!"

Pierre narrowed his gaze on Beau, then grinned at Jesse. "It won't matter in the long run."

Jesse stood like a man ready to fight, his large fists balled and shoulders tense. Her head still on the argument regarding her countrymen and the losses in France, Lorraine could have spanked the men for their squabbling. Pierre's comment cooled her, though, and when she met Jesse's gaze, she found the group in a square, with her and Jesse on one side and Beau and Pierre on the other.

She would not let him die, not after glimpsing his heart in the cave. If he'd called for help, he might have lived and not have to endure Pierre's ominous threats. For now, though, she needed to keep the peace, especially since it was Beau and not Pierre whom Jesse faced.

The train whistle sounded off in the distance. Like the sun breaking through clouds, it brought her reprieve from the storm. "We are wasting time. I will see you at the end of the line." She met Beau's gaze, and upon receiving his nod, Lorraine mounted her horse and rode through the stream alone.

∼

*T*he Utah Northern Railroad train rattled along the track, dusty and loud from the compact passenger car. Lorraine straightened her neck, the weariness in her body pulling hard. She wished to rest beside the window, but her straw hat and hatpin prevented such. Besides, a train was hardly a place to slumber, especially when she was part of a group of kidnappers. She pinched the tips of her kid gloves, shipped from France—the one luxury she afforded herself—and then ran her finger down the smooth cotton seams of her bodice. The light-blue dress was relatively simple, even with its embroidered black trim, but after her men's britches and six-gun, she felt as though she'd donned the gown of a queen. She had stashed the clothing in Franklin over a week ago on her way to Cariboo Mountain. It made for the perfect disguise—modest, simple, and unremarkable.

Outlaw. Liar. Bandit. Selfish. Jesse's accusations rang from memory, forcing an ache into her chest. He had seemed determined to guilt her about kidnapping him, yet he'd argued for the sake of others, not himself. He was right. She'd robbed others. And she was right. His kind had liberty and riches to spare, unlike her people.

Even now the Americans crowded around, an especially loud group behind her. She pressed herself against the dirty wall. The troupe she grew up with was plenty loud, but she had belonged with them, not in America.

A large man in coveralls stood behind her and spoke to someone across the aisle. He'd offered to help her with her bag when she found her seat, but she'd waved him off. Now he gripped the back of her bench to steady himself, catching her hair in the process. The sharp tug held her in place. She was caught, head back and tongue useless. If she spoke, she would reveal her nationality and be all the more memorable if something went wrong. What could she do? Her feet scraped the floor, breathlessness—as though she was being smothered—flooding over her.

The man moved his hand, and the tension ceased. Lorraine stood and strode toward the door, her carpetbag abandoned on the floor. Rows of strangers stared ahead. At her. They would see her, recognize her, and hunt her down.

Two little girls sat like a pair of large-eyed owls on a limb.

They brightened upon noticing her, but Lorraine avoided them. Their mother dozed with her own hat over her face, the creases of dirt in her dress revealing that they had traveled far.

Lorraine bumped her hip against a bench. When a ruffle of her dress caught on a splinter, the hiss of fabric told her of some damage, but Lorraine kept moving. She stepped onto the vestibule platform, hot air hitting her moist temples.

The wheels thundered on the rails, and dust stirred around her. Catching up her dress, she hopped across the gap and onto the stock car. There she rapped the code she and Beau had made together as children.

Sure enough, the door swung open, and there stood her friend, his tired countenance shadowed by worry.

"Too many people." She spoke loudly enough for him to grasp her words, yet when she spotted Jesse sitting on the floor with bound hands between his knees, she hoped he had not heard. Since he'd spoken so sincerely in her ear, urging her to live, she'd struggled to meet his gaze.

He focused on her with an irresistible pull. "Lorraine, stopping by for a visit, hmm?" He spoke in English, not the French she preferred. "Sorry, I can't offer you a chair."

Jesse's anger had bubbled beneath the surface since they left the cave. Did he regret not calling to the farmers for help?

Beau pulled out a stool for her, then sank down to the opposite wall. Several farm animals gathered at the rear of the car, hay laid down as bedding. He blinked tiredly and adjusted his hat. "As long as you're here, mind if I take a nap?"

"Not at all."

Her friend pushed his hat low and sat still.

"So you own a dress?" Jesse ran his fingers through his hair, though hostility still emulated from him. "Could I get these ropes cut?"

She raised an eyebrow.

"I'm not going to jump off a moving train with my hands tied."

Glancing away, Lorraine flattened her mouth. "I think you are quite capable of doing that."

Beau scoffed. "It's a good way to break an arm."

Jesse smirked. "You speak from experience?"

Beau met her gaze.

"Lorraine?" Jesse laughed, though the sound was not kind. "How did you come to do that? A robbery, I suppose."

Her childhood friend glared at Jesse. "No. It was a prisoner train, actually, and none of your business."

"Prison? Why am I not surprised?"

"Lorrie did nothing deserving of imprisonment, and neither did any of the other people on that train!"

This was hardly the time or place to open those terrible old wounds. Her arms still ached when the weather turned cold, reminding her every year of the escape and those she'd left behind.

"Beau, non. Leave it be. He has a right to his anger. Imagine how you would feel if you were in his position. We took him. He has done nothing to warrant such treatment."

"You don't know anything about this man! Emil arranged the robbery on his mine with specific directions to take Jesse alive. He wouldn't do that without a good reason."

"Pierre is lying about Jesse. Just trying to get more money, greedy man."

"He's not, Lorrie." Beau sat forward, his legs crossed. "You might as well know, because Jesse is not getting away on my watch. I was there, before we left Salt Lake. Emil chose you for the robbery only because he wanted this kid alive, and he knew you would make sure that happened."

Lorraine disagreed with the shake of her head. "If that is true, why did you agree to come back with me when I said I thought Pierre was up to something? We had already gotten rid of the gold."

Beau bunched his chin and shrugged.

There had to be a misunderstanding. Emil would not set her up to kidnap someone. But then...he hadn't. She wasn't supposed to know about Jesse. Her mistrust of Pierre had led her to the truth. Jesse returned her gaze, his face placid, though doubtless he plotted, gleaning as much information from the conversation as possible to use toward an escape.

"Are you a thief?" she demanded of him. "Were you or your father involved in something nefarious, dishonest? Perhaps with his mine?"

Jesse glared. "I'm an honest man. As is my father. Unlike the two of you. I'd wager you are both wanted." Color grew in his neck, and he slammed his feet on the floor, straining against his bonds and causing muscles in his arms and shoulders to bulge. "Let me go!"

The train rattled and vibrated, reminding her of that cold, dank stock car they had stuffed her into at the end of the Bloody Week. She closed her eyes, Jesse's shouts sending her deeper into the past.

"You have no right. Let me go!"

All of a sudden, the car jolted violently, bouncing Lorraine on the stool. She covered her face, the scent of feces, sweat, and death all around her.

A roar sounded. Metal screeched.

She was thrown to the floor, then the whole car flipped, rolling her onto the wall. Jesse fell into a similar position, the hay and animals tumbling onto the now-vertical wall behind him. The side of the car rumbled. Dragged on the ground.

Panting, Lorraine struggled to her hands and knees.

Just as she rose, a large crate fell, pinning her in place.

CHAPTER 5

The wall beneath Jesse trembled like an earthquake as the car dragged on its side. The roar of wood scraping over rocks filled his ears. Lorraine lay beneath the crate. He pressed his palms to the wooden siding, trying to rise from the position he'd fallen into. His uncoordinated scramble landed him on his belly.

Beau rolled over in front of him, reaching for Lorraine.

Silence fell and the shaking ceased. A goat bleated loudly. The cows fought to untangle themselves, one having torn the bar it had been tied to. The bovines' hooves beat the wall, their lowing filling the cab. If they came any nearer, they'd trample all three of the people for sure.

Beau strained to lift his head, blood pouring from a gash near his hairline. When he shifted, the sheathed knife on his belt came into view. Jesse seized it, staked it between his unbound feet, and sawed through his bonds, barely aware of the throbbing in his wrists and raw skin. Lorraine remained unmoving. How badly was she hurt? He sawed harder.

"Lorrie!" The name came out slurred as Beau tried to gain his feet yet fell again.

Free from the bonds, Jesse grabbed hold of Beau. "Whoa, Beau. You've got a head wound. Just sit before you bleed out." He searched Beau's saddle pack and found an old shirt. The cattle continued to complain, one flailing when it tried to stand and its leg gave way. Another pulled at its rope. The goats jumped around, butting heads and ramming into the wall. One came for Jesse. He pushed it away and wrapped Beau's head with the shirt, tying the sleeves to secure it.

"Lorrie!" Beau called more clearly now, and when he groaned loudly, she turned.

"Beau?" She struggled beneath the weight of the container, her knuckles white as she tried to push it off.

Jesse knelt at her side and lifted the obstruction, then froze, his gaze locked with Lorraine's. Her eyes shone with fear, and blood dripped from her nose. "Jesse, please..."

What was he doing? This was his chance to escape. Beau had received a blow to the head, and Lorraine was trapped. He'd not seen Pierre since they'd parted ways by the creek, but he'd bet money the man was somewhere on the train. And Jesse wasn't waiting to be found. He'd not called for help in the cave for Lorraine's sake, but what about Aubrey? She needed him to return home, and Lorraine was preventing that.

Jesse lifted just enough for her to wiggle free, which she did and without a backward glance, crawled toward Beau. "Come, we must move you before the beasts get loose and trample you to death. Lean on me, *mon chéri*."

Beau slung an arm over her shoulders, but the two struggled and collapsed. They needed help, but Beau would see Jesse dead before he let him escape. Jesse gained the train car door and worked the lever. It fell open, hanging on its hinges. He squeezed sideways through, into the dusty air.

Jesse stumbled on solid ground, his legs trembling from the shock. Several cars lay on their sides. Shards of wood and metal littered the rutted ground where the cars had been dragged.

The railroad tracks cut through the surrounding rocky hills. The trek to Franklin would be long, but he could telegraph Pa from there.

He hiked up the tracks, the wind, his pulse, and the moaning of the injured cow filling his ears. Jesse stretched his legs, breaking into a run. His muscles ached with stiffness yet warmed with the motion, his heart beating the tempo of freedom. The continuous rumble in his ears grew, and a strange smell scented the air.

A gunshot blasted.

He jerked around. The locomotive and the passenger car were strewn beside the track, the latter engulfed in flames and black smoke. Beau sat in the shade of the overturned stock car, holding his head as Lorraine emerged with her pistol. The animal no longer bellowed, so she must have put it out of its misery. She faced the burning train like a man ready to fight.

What was she thinking? "Lorraine!" She wouldn't actually run into such danger alone, would she? "Lorraine, don't!" He started back the way he'd come, unable to leave the crash without helping. "Lorraine!"

The woman took off, skirts billowing behind her.

"Lorraine, wait!" Jesse broke into a run, racing past Beau. The roar of the blaze grew and screams of passengers filled his ears. Lorraine reached the burning car and tossed her gun. Two men struggled through the horizontal doorway, carrying a wounded man between them. As soon as they cleared the doorway, Lorraine girded up her skirts.

"Lorraine, stop!" He pumped his arms and legs faster, but she disappeared inside.

He followed her in, ducking low through the narrow opening. A big man in overalls shoved Jesse toward a boy about fifteen who was struggling to pull an unconscious older man from between debris. Some of the benches hung from the floor, having not been secure enough to stay connected and having fallen on top of passengers.

"Here, let me take his arms. You grab his feet." He gripped the elderly man, who was as heavy as an ox, and began moving him. The kid did his best, his eyes bright in his dirty face.

Outside, black smoke swept past the windows. Jesse adjusted his grip when he came to the sideways door and climbed through.

"Watch his head," a man called, and took Jesse's place. "We'll move him away from the fire. There's a bit of shade by the stream. We need to move everyone over there."

"Yes, sir." Jesse helped the kid through, then entered the train again.

People lay on the wall, strewn at odd angles. Many were bloodied and dazed. Several benches lodged together in a tangle, barricading people closest to the engine on the other side of the car. Shattered glass and splintered wood littered the place. Two little girls knelt beside a very pale lady with a blood-soaked blouse. Lorraine crouched with them.

"Non. Do not cry." Lorraine's heavily accented voice was strong but tender. She ripped ruffles from her petticoats and pressed them to the mother's wounded arm. "Be strong, *ma chérie*. Press the cloth here."

"Grab this, son." A big farmer wrestled with a large board that locked the tangle of benches into a heap.

"Help! It's hot. The fire!" Those closest to the flames cried out amid the roar of the blaze.

Jesse went to the farmer's side, and together they removed the obstruction. Several benches tumbled forward. The other men scrambled to control the movement and ensure no one else got hurt.

The rescuers formed a line, carrying pieces of the wreckage out. People stumbled through the mayhem, some bloody and others helping the women and children. All the while, Jesse kept an eye on Lorraine.

Finally, the way was clear and only a few passengers remained. Sweat wet his hair, chest, and back, but Jesse kept working, moving heavy pieces and carrying those who couldn't walk. The fire gripped one end of the car, heat and smoke filtering in. Lorraine stayed near the lady with her daughters, having bandaged the wound and secured her injured arm in a makeshift splint. The girls no longer cried, though they were dusty and scraped up themselves. They worked well under Lorraine's direction.

Outside, Jesse settled a man on the ground, waiting for others to carry him into the shelter of the trees. The girls who had been with Lorraine clambered out into the sunlight. They looked around in confusion.

"Girls, come. The fire is growing." He grasped their tiny hands and pulled them away.

A man came to the door, supporting the girls' mother beneath the arms while Lorraine struggled through the doorway, gripping the lady's knees. "Jesse, she needs to be carried, gently. Take her?"

He lifted her, and Lorraine adjusted her head so it would not fall. "She has a broken arm and a piece of wood in her side. You must walk steadily, careful not to jolt her."

He met her clear, dark gaze, finding open concern there. A deep pull moved him toward her. He should say something. She'd been courageous and strong, and now she looked so alive —fierce with her wild hair, sure stance, torn dress, and scratches. He wanted to clasp her in his arms. Turn her in a circle and tell her how brave she was. Instead, he headed for the grove of trees where people took shelter.

In reality, Lorraine was his enemy, not his friend. He needed to remember that and avoid her—now, before Beau and Pierre showed up and attempted to capture him again.

~

*C*ool spring water slipped between Lorraine's fingers, washing away the grime and blood. The branches of mighty fir trees swayed above, settling spears of light around her and the wounded resting in their shelter. Lorraine eased onto a downed log on the sandy soil.

The fire was under control at last, though many of the men still hurried along the tracks and splashed the locomotive with buckets of water to ensure all coals had indeed been doused. Though the boiler had not exploded, the coal man, who had been stoking the fire when the accident occurred, was knocked unconscious. When he awoke, the open furnace had spilled its contents. There had been farming equipment transported in the last car, behind the stock cars. Someone used those to clear the land in an attempt to contain the fire, then finally, men from nearby farms must have seen the smoke, because help arrived.

Several of the horses that had been in a different stock car than Lorraine had died, including Beau's. Pierre's horse and Silvia were nowhere to be seen, like Beau and Pierre. Had Beau taken her horse? She wouldn't necessarily blame him, but he'd left her behind.

The wounded lady Lorraine had helped was resting, her bleeding mostly stopped. She huddled with her daughters in the shade, the slanting of the sun signaling that twilight would soon call this day to an end. Some of the men had returned to the shade of the trees. Jesse walked between two men his age, his shirt torn and burned, hair mussed beneath his hat, and his gaze fixed decidedly away from her. Would he turn her in as soon as he got the chance?

An elderly lady approached Lorraine, offering her a cup of water. "Oh, Miss—well, I don't even know your name."

Biting her lip, Lorraine forced her best English. "Mrs. Lorrie

Michel." The surname was a common French name with Hebrew origins.

"Mrs. Michel, a lovely name. I'm Elizabeth Jones." Madam Jones shook Lorraine's hand, her skin soft and face kind. "You have a beautiful accent. How long have you been in our country?"

"This last year."

"And you are traveling alone?" Concern showed from Mrs. Jones's face.

"Yes, but I will soon meet with my husband in Salt Lake City." Hopefully, that would satisfy the woman' curiosity.

"My sons have caught grouse. Will you join us for dinner?"

To refuse would draw more attention to her. "*Merci beaucoup.*"

Lorraine followed the elderly lady to a fire with four well-placed spits over it. If she knew Beau, he'd return for her. But what if he'd suffered an aneurysm because of his head injury? And what of Pierre? The man would never leave a job unfinished. Should she warn Jesse?

Madam Jones bent over the fire, turning a number of grouses on spits. Lorraine pressed bare fingers together, her gloves having been ruined in the crash. It was so odd to have the lady cook for her, but Madam Jones would not let her lift a finger.

She motioned toward the swiftly flowing creek. "I can get water."

"No need, mademoiselle." One of the men who walked with Jesse strode up, offering Madam Jones a bucket of water and Lorraine a grin.

The introductions were made, though Lorraine hardly heard any of the names as Jesse drew nearer.

Madam Jones patted Jesse's arm. "And this fine young man is Mr. Jesse Alexander, of Los Angeles, California. He made friends with my grandsons while working on that fire. Jesse, this sweet lady is Mrs. Michel. She's recently come over from France and is going to meet her husband in Salt Lake City."

"Mrs. Michel." Jesse shook her hand, his clean palm firm and warm, the rope burns of his wrists reminding her of the power he now held.

Barely able to maintain his narrowed gaze, Lorraine greeted him in French, her voice painfully timid. Her sins were sure to find her out.

All through the meal, people came from the nearby town, transporting those worse off than Madam Jones's family. Lorraine tried to avoid conversation, feigning linguistic confusion, though the friendly Americans just tried harder to communicate with her. With every attempt, their voices grew louder, as if she also suffered hearing loss. The tension stretched tighter when Jesse offered to interpret. Finally, the meal was over and she excused herself to find a moment of privacy.

Away from the others, Lorraine drew in a deep, cleansing breath. The trees were matted with the vines of wood roses, and she picked a bunch as she ventured downstream. The sun was still hot, though it was leaning near the horizon. With the air heavily scented with sage and cool waters trickling past, Lorraine settled herself on the dirty bank and unbuttoned her boots. She didn't dare remove her stockings but soaked them with her feet in the cool water. Next, she pulled out the pins she'd used to secure a chignon at the base of her neck, massaging her scalp. She was far enough away from others to not be seen in such an inappropriate state.

When all was done, she sat trying to clear her thoughts. They had been a whirl since the day Emil had come to the Sells Brothers Circus back East and proposed a plan that would provide more gold for their people than the small bits of her earnings she had been sending since coming to America. The robbery was supposed to be a way to make a difference. Jesse's capture had changed everything, and now today—the crash and fire.

She ached for the mother and her two daughters, who had been among the first to be moved to a nearby town. She'd learned their surname was Sinclair and they had been on their way to visit Mr. Sinclair. Lord willing, Mrs. Sinclair would recover soon and the family be reunited. The girls were so young, as was their mother. Too young to die. At least too good to die, unlike Lorraine, who had no loved ones and had sank low into criminal life. A far cry from the woman her maman and *Père* wanted her to be.

What was she doing here? She should be in Salt Lake. No. She should be in Paris with Maman. But she was dead, and Paris would never be the same.

I don't belong anywhere.

"Lorraine? Lorraine, where are you?" Jesse strode through the sagebrush behind her, looking around, only to halt at the sight of her.

She hid her feet beneath her skirt, but he still stared at her as though he'd spotted a pelican in the desert. Lorraine swiped up her boots.

He motioned for her to stay. "You needn't rise. I will sit. We need to talk." He lowered himself beside her, yet his manner was decidedly distant. "What is your plan, now that Beau and Pierre have abandoned you?"

Lorraine stiffened and crumpled the flowers.

"That's right, I saw them ride out of here, not offering to help anyone."

"Beau was hurt."

"Not so hurt that he couldn't sit a horse. Your horse."

"Beau will come back for me." Lorraine unfolded her fingers, revealing wilted roses with crushed pieces. She removed the stems and gently set the blossoms in the stream, where they floated like happy little boats.

"What are you doing?" Jesse's irritated voice broke into her solace, and she startled.

"Making fairy boats."

His brow relaxed a little. "They're not boats. They're...well, we always called them water lilies."

"'We'?"

"My maman taught my sister and me to remove the stems so just the blossoms float on the water. She called them water lilies."

"My maman taught me the same thing. Only she called them fairy boats. But I suppose fairies might use lily pads for boats." She quirked the sides of her mouth. After all, Jesse was free, and Beau was gone for now.

He grasped a nearby reed and fiddled with the end. "Is it true, your family is all dead?"

She nodded and turned to making more water lilies.

Sun rays slipped past him, catching on his firm jaw when he turned his head to face her more fully. "How did you end up being a thief?"

"Must we speak? I am tired."

"You don't think I deserve to know why I was shot at, knocked unconscious, trussed up, and dragged across the country?"

"You were not shot at. The men used slingshots to take down the rear guards, using rocks that landed without serious injury. I climbed in the wagon and struck you and the driver. There was no shooting. That is a rule of mine."

"A rule of yours? You've been waving your gun at me for days."

"Because you attacked me that first night. You pose a danger to me. Regardless, I decided it would be better to be the victim than cause further harm when we were in the cave. It takes courage to welcome pain. I'm not even justified in defending myself because I'm an outlaw."

"And whose fault is that?"

"It is mine. I know. I am wrong!" She'd fallen far from polite society and lost herself along the way. Jesse was the first person to reprimand her. The first person to care. She splashed water on her hot cheeks. "As for why you were kidnapped, that I do not know. You've heard me argue with Pierre. You heard what Beau said today. It is more likely you know the reason than I do."

"If that's true, why didn't you help me get free?"

"You attacked me. Tried to hurt me. Even if I thought I had good reason to betray my people, which I could never do, it would be dangerous." Her throat hardened, and tears born from an exhausted mind and body threatened. "Don't think you're the first man who's looked at me and seen only prey."

He glared, but the expression fell like a mask. In its place was an embarrassed young man who needed a shave and a good night's sleep. "I guess I can't blame you for that, but this is the life you chose. A bad life where you'll encounter bad men and come to a bad end, Lorraine."

"I never wanted this life. There is no room for me in this land—your perfect America. I miss my home to which I can never return." Fighting tears again, she threw a handful of the flowers into the stream. They sailed just as quickly as the pretty ones, making their way to rougher waters where waves over-whelmed and drowned them.

Jesse tossed his reed in after them. "You are not safe, and I won't just stand by while you trust ruthless men who will play you false. You are suffering now, but your life will get worse."

"Worse? I am a stranger in a strange land. All my family dead and my only friend gone."

"True, but you are strong. Your spirit is not crushed...yet."

"What do you know of my spirit? You are so concerned, but you won't see me again. I will have to go on alone if Beau is badly hurt."

Color grew in his cheeks. "I've seen what happens to a woman when she trusts the wrong sort of man. When her spirit is broken. I do not want that for you."

"Why do you say that?" Her throat went dry. "Do you know someone who was thus broken?"

He swallowed hard, his tan jaw twitching when he answered through his teeth. "My sister, Aubrey. She fell in love with a wealthy banker. He said all the right things, but there was something about the way he spoke to her and hovered over her in the presence of other men. Even me, her brother. I thought something wasn't right, but she said she loved him. My mother had just died. I was expelled from school when I failed mathematics. I returned and graduated with full honors, but for a while, I was so disheartened. At the time, it felt like my life was over. I didn't trust myself."

Jesse had struggled so. And he'd lost his mother. The sinking feeling in Lorraine's stomach took the fire right out of her. Perhaps they had more in common than she realized. "What happened?"

His shoulders sagged. "I didn't say anything. Aubrey married him and moved away. I was alone in our big house. My pa was away on business. I closed myself up in my study and went to a dark place in my mind. Aubrey wrote me letters. They helped to keep me afloat, but when they stopped, I sank deeper until every day was misery, seemingly without end."

She slipped her fingers into his. "Even when you have a good life, things can seem utterly dark. What happened?"

He studied their clasped hands, her petite fingertips between his, then ran his thumb across her skin.

Warmth unfurled inside her like the gentle budding of a spring blossom. Did he know what he was doing to her?

Likely not, for he continued, "Aubrey wrote me, telling me that she would be in Salt Lake with her husband. I met her there, and she told me the truth, that he was cruel and unfaithful. She wanted to come home, but when I tried to help, some of his friends gave me a good whipping. I never felt so helpless in my life." He gritted his teeth yet drew in a deep breath "My pa has a friend who's a federal marshal. He lives in Salt Lake, and I was staying with him. He told me Aubrey's husband was suspected of fraud, but they lacked proof. I broke into his office and got the paperwork proving this. Left the paper for the officer to find and didn't tell anyone. It was illegal, after all. The police arrested him, and I took Aubrey home, but she was never the same. She's a shell of the woman she was, even though I try to help her."

"And I kept you from her." She loosened her fingers.

"Actually, my pa did when he forced me to go to our mine on Cariboo Mountain. I had served my time at Pa's mine and was going home when you robbed the shipment. That was why I was riding guard. Because I was going home—or rather, to Grays Lake."

"Why there?"

"We used to stop there to fish and picnic when our mother was alive." A smile softened his features. "Aubrey had a love for photography. I got her a big camera, hoping to get her interested. We had a deal that if I could take a photo clear enough to see the whole lake, she would do me a favor."

"What favor?"

"A trip abroad. She'd always wanted to go to Europe, but she married instead. We were supposed to go to France with our mother to visit family. I thought it might wake her up, bring her back to herself for a bit."

"How long has she been like that?"

"Six months."

"She likely needs more time to process and heal, feel safe. After being abused and betrayed by her husband..." She snapped her gaze to his. "You cannot heal her, though, Jesse.

You must know that. We don't gain healing from others. It's inside, in time, with God."

"I'm surprised to hear an outlaw talk about God."

"I wasn't always an outlaw."

He shifted his feet, stirring up dust. "It's true—I can't heal her, but I need to help her. It's my fault she ended up in such a bad way."

"Nonsense. Why, even if you had warned her, if the woman thought herself in love, it is likely nothing would have stopped her. How old was she?"

"Twenty at the time. She is three years older than me."

"Your father did not warn her?"

Jesse thumbed his stubble-laden chin. "Likely, he did. But that is beside the point. I failed to protect my sister."

"You fail to see the point." She raised a hand, silencing him. "You rescued her. You have loved her and put her first. God will use you to bring her out of her darkness—if she desires to be free."

A slight breeze flittered over the water, swiping curls past her cheeks and waving the top of Jesse's hair.

"Why would she not wish to be free?"

"Sometimes we wallow in our misery before finding a reason to return to ourselves. I hope you see her soon and that she has the victory over her past. Time. She will need a lot of it."

He rubbed his face roughly before giving her his bloodshot gaze.

Lorraine squirmed, a flutter in her middle warning her to lean back. Jesse was handsome, honest, and strong. Yielding to the ache for connection would be easy...but fruitless. If only they'd met under different circumstances. But here they were at a crossroads, going their separate ways. "What will you do, Jesse?"

"Do you mean, will I turn you in?" He cocked an eyebrow.

Heat rushing to her cheeks, she spoke quickly. "I just meant, do you need money to telegraph your father or..." He smirked, and Lorraine shrugged. "I'm sorry." He didn't need to remind her of her wrong. His raw wrists, head wound, and bruises were enough. "I never should have let them take you, or gone along with them after you frightened me."

"I didn't plan to hurt you, Lorraine. I just needed to be free, and I thought you were my best option."

She nodded, pinching her lips together.

"As for going along with them, I thought you trusted this Emil person." His voice hardened again.

"I don't know who I trust. I just know it was wrong." Here she'd been fighting because her people had lost their liberty, and she'd taken Jesse's in the process. "I have salve in my bags I can get for your wrists." Lorraine stood.

Jesse did as well, objecting to the offer.

She took a step, coming down on something sharp in the creek bed. With a yelp, she hopped to one side.

Jesse took her arms, switching to English when he spoke. "What's wrong?"

"I must have stepped on a thorn."

"May I see?"

Her foot? Without a shoe? Good heavens, how scandalous. Even as the thoughts dawned, she nodded her consent. He guided her to sit once again, then brushed aside the cotton hem of her dress. The white stockings were dirty and wet, yet the warmth of his suntanned hands still soaked through the fabric.

"Here we are." He pinched off a thorn and tossed it into the stream.

"Thank you." She pulled her foot away.

He was closer now than ever, the blue depths of his eyes like a stormy sea. "I shouldn't have hesitated to help you when you were under that crate."

"You needed to escape. I'd have done the same thing to you."

He chuckled and drew one leg up to prop an arm on it. "Are you an only child, then?"

Why was he carrying the conversation here? "Why do you ask about my family?"

He answered in English. "When you grow up with siblings, you learn to look after others."

"I see. I am an only child. My father died before I was born, and my mother swore to never remarry."

"A shame."

"Why is that a shame? And won't you please speak French?"

"It's a shame because if she had, maybe you would not have been left alone when she died. Why don't you speak my language when I have spoken yours for the last few days?"

Aching a little more because of his comments, she raised her chin. "If Maman had other children, they, too, would likely be dead, and I do not wish to speak English because I find solace in the language of my country while I'm forced to abide living in yours."

"You do not know that they would have died. If you don't like America, return to France. As for which language you speak, why not do something for someone else for a change? Only speaking French because you are comfortable doing so is selfish. You should have at least tried to converse with Mrs. Jones."

Lorraine clenched her teeth. How dare he tell her to go back to France? If only she could. She looked away, only to catch sight of Mrs. Jones peering concernedly in her direction. She was a kind lady.

Lorraine licked her lips and tried her best at his language. "You are right. I am selfish. Mrs. Jones is kind. I do not belong in this land, but I cannot return home, regardless of how much I wish to set foot in France once again."

"Might that be dangerous for you?"

"No. There is some semblance of peace there, and I am of no real note to anyone there save my Roma family. I wish to know if they are still alive." She clenched handfuls of her skirt, squeezing as her chest compressed with pain, until finally she could breathe again. "As for English, I speak very—how do you say?—ah, poorly."

"I can't say where you belong, but since you are planted in American soil, why not try to grow good roots and bloom?" He lifted a stray rose from the dirt and tucked it behind her ear. "As for speaking my language, you do so beautifully. I think I could listen to you for hours."

He held his hand near her cheek. Before he could touch her, Lorraine gently covered his, her fingertips warmed by the contact. She returned it to him, her insides twisting with loneliness. "Please, do not be sweet to me."

He sighed. "You're right. We'll both go our separate ways now."

"And even if we did not..." She shook her head. "Impossible."

For a moment, there was only the stirring of the leaves in the trees, then the rattle of wagon wheels in the distance.

"People have come from the nearby towns, offering to take in passengers for the night." Jesse stood, donning his hat. "There are two wagons coming. Looks like one from Franklin and the other from the town farther down the line. You going forward or back?"

"Forward, to the next town." What other way was there?

"Fair enough. I will go back to Franklin. Should be a telegram office there, and I can contact my father. Beau and Pierre will expect me to go back, but I will alert the sheriff. He'll watch for strangers in town." He scraped his worn boots in the dirt, stirring up dust that floated around her, causing her to sneeze.

"*Excuse-moi.* I did not mean to kick dust at you." He shrugged, cheeks red.

He so resembled a boy within the man that she permitted a smile. "It's nothing. Now turn so I can don my shoes."

He gave her his back—his strong, broad back. The wind was kind and pressed the fabric of his shirt against contoured muscles.

Lorraine hurried with the buttons on her boots. Such thoughts were fruitless for so many reasons. Why admire him when they had no future? She'd not thought of a future with any man since her school days. Since mama told her she should marry a French gentleman and not one of their troupe. Jesse was half American, though, which might actually make him less suitable.

She pulled down her hem and rose to her feet. "All right. I am presentable now."

He turned, only to shake his head. "Except for your hair, right?"

"Oh." She clasped the long black curls and wove them into a braid. "I took it down only to allow myself some protection from the sun."

"Well, it's...ah..." He followed her ministrations with his gaze, then blinked and shook his head. "The sun has nearly set now."

"Yes, I noticed. Thank you, though."

He grinned and offered his arm as she secured the last pin into her chignon. "You're welcome."

Walking beside him like a proper lady suited them so well. Who would have thought she'd be smitten by the young man she'd seen unconscious and bleeding in the back of the wagon full of gold? If Pierre hadn't taken Jesse, she'd have never known him. No matter the hardships they'd faced, such an acquaintance seemed a treasure.

~

*C*itrine glowed from the hill tops. The day was ending, at last. Jesse glanced over his shoulder, his muscles aching after such hard days. It was difficult to believe it was almost over—the crash, the kidnapping, and being so far away from Aubrey. The woods on the other side of the creek were quiet, but Pierre and Beau might be waiting there. He'd have to be extra vigilant to avoid capture again.

Was it true that Lorraine's boss ordered his kidnapping? But why try from so far away? After all, he was going back to California, which was a longer journey from Salt Lake than Idaho. It must have been coincidence that he was taken, as Lorraine suspected. Once he arrived at a law office, he would connect with his funds and hire gunmen. No traveling alone.

A few passengers remained, most having been carted away by nearby settlers who knew the meaning of being neighborly in the wilderness.

Mrs. Jones was still with Lorraine, who stooped over the saddlebags and a carpetbag he'd lugged off the train for her. The ladies conversed, Mrs. Jones pointing to the rose behind Lorraine's ear. The corners of her pretty lips peaked on one side. She touched the bud as she looked around...for him?

So beautiful. Angelic, and even more so when she met his gaze and flushed. Jesse's cheeks tightened, though he tried to bite back a smile. He had no time for foolish notions of romance. Touching her so gently, taking such a liberty at the stream, had been a mistake. They had no future, and flirting with danger could get him tied up again. No matter what, he could not trust Lorraine completely. Only a fool would.

Lorraine lifted her gun belt from her things but stored it back in a leather bag. Next, her Stetson hat went into place, and her shoulders straightened. He drew near as Lorraine spoke in her broken English to Mrs. Jones. Her voice was soft—not timid, but a little uncertain. She misspoke, and the lady laughed. Lorraine blushed furiously and shrugged, lifting her gaze to meet his.

All that was shadowy about her countenance lightened, as though a full moon kissed her skin. "Jesse?" The soul-deep warmth in her voice quickened his heart but also brought a quick frown to Mrs. Jones's face.

Well, what could be expected when Lorraine had claimed to be a married woman? What if he could court her? Would she always be a liar, or was that something she did to survive? She'd been educated to be a lady, and he'd seen a more cultured side of her in the stock car before the crash. Lorraine, clad in a lady's blue traveling suit with buttons up the front to a ruffled collar, had moved with grace, seating herself on the stool as though ascending to a velvet settee. Her posture, proud as always, had also hinted at modesty. He liked her best now, in long, feminine skirts, the jacket gone, leaving her in the white shirtwaist, and a tan Stetson contrasting with her midnight-black hair.

Forcing polite restraint into his voice for appearance's sake, he bowed slightly to her. "May I have a word with you, Mrs. Michel?"

She blinked, likely remembering where she was and the pretense they must keep. "Certainly."

"Hold on a minute." Mrs. Jones crossed her arms. "That is a mite improper, young man. Asking to speak alone with a married woman. And this is after you sought her out by the creek." She took Lorraine by the arm. "She is new to our land and vulnerable. Do you wish to take advantage of her with your good looks and ability to speak her language?"

Lorraine's eyes grew large. She'd likely not expected the kindness and was struck dumb. He'd have to get out of this scrape on his own.

"I appreciate your protectiveness, Mrs. Jones, but I'm afraid we haven't been completely honest. You see, Lorrie and I were acquainted before this meeting."

She pulled Lorraine farther away, shielding her. "How so?"

"She is my wife." His heart thundered in his ears. The elderly lady bristled, but Lorraine was utterly still.

Mrs. Jones looked between the two of them. "Why lie about such a thing?"

"I am not a good woman." Lorraine spoke quietly. "Jesse rescued me from a bad situation. We had to travel separate because some people from my past are looking for me. They know we ran off together, so we are less conspicuous apart."

Mrs. Jones frowned before softening. "I am sorry, my dear. I sensed you were hiding something. I can help you both, though. Where are you headed from here?"

"I lost some supplies on the wreck and need to return to Franklin to the mercantile." Jesse covered Lorraine's hand, and she moved so quickly against him that her skirts brushed his legs. "If you could see her to Ogden, I will follow in a day or so."

"Of course, I will. Now, you two say your goodbyes. We need to leave soon." And with that, she swished away.

Lorraine slowly lifted her gaze to him, her grip on his arm easing. "I'm sorry you felt you had to lie. That must not be easy for you."

"Is it easy for you?" He turned to shelter her from the woods which might contain those willing to hurt her because of their intimate proximity.

Cheeks turning rosy, she glanced down, then up again. "Lying has become easier over the years, though my maman raised me to be honest. She took a switch to my back when I lied, saying if I was not honest, I would lose myself. I suppose that is part of the reason I framed our lie to Mrs. Jones as near the truth as it could be."

"Our lie." He hated that the first thing they shared was a sin.

If it were true, he'd have the right to protect her. "I don't wish you ill, Lorraine. I wish you freedom and a life absent pain."

"No life is absent pain."

"True, but no one should have to walk through it alone." As Aubrey did, despite his constantly trying to help carry her load. She simply hadn't wanted him. He hadn't been enough to protect Aubrey. He wouldn't be enough for Lorraine either.

Lacing his fingers through hers, he drew in a deep breath. "Earlier, you sounded as though you might regret this life. What will it take for you to change your way of living?"

"You meeting me in Ogden?" She raised her eyebrows, a jaunty little smile not matching the flicker of hope in her eyes. Before he could respond, she continued. "As a matter of fact, I was talking to Mrs. Jones. She said there are some positions as maids in the bigger cities, but since I am educated, I might be a governess."

Head still whirling from the suggestion they meet in Ogden, Jesse managed a steady reply. "You were good with the girls on the train."

"They are very sweet, aren't they?"

He nodded. "What would you need to get started?"

"Work history, which I do not have, just as I do not have proof of my education, though the school is well known. It might be enough. If only my English was better."

"Perhaps you should practice more." He smiled and then so did she, wetting her lips before speaking his language.

"I have not had so many, how do you say..."—she furrowed her brow—"opportune?"

"You have not had many opportunities."

"Oui, until meeting you."

He resisted the urge to run his thumb across her knuckles. He had to do this right, though. Needed to give Lorraine hope that she could make it on her own, because he wasn't meeting her after this. His duty was to Aubrey and Pa, the latter of whom would insist an investigation be carried out. Lorraine, if she started a new life, might avoid being caught. How could he influence her to truly change her life permanently? "Lorraine, is this real?"

"What do you mean?"

"I mean, this plan of being a governess? Of changing your life? Staying away from people like Pierre and whoever your boss is? To live honestly?"

"Live honestly, yes. But first, I have business with Emil that is not finished."

"What business is more important than your life? The men you are riding with are dangerous, no matter how fast your draw. That's not enough. They will just shoot you in the back when you are not looking."

Gaze lowering, she shrugged. "Emil made a deal with me, to do something very important if I worked this job for him."

"You have no guarantee he will. Going to Salt Lake City won't ensure that happens. If this man is as honest as you say, won't he keep his word to you regardless?"

"Of course he would."

"Then you needn't contact him and be sucked back into that life. I'm telling you, you need to stay away from those people. Pierre and Beau are gone. You could disappear, find a job. Make a new life. Be someone different."

Mrs. Jones called from the wagon, waving for Lorraine to join them. Everything was loaded, and several people already sat in the open buckboard with a farmer at the reins.

"I will try to find a way out." She dragged her fingers from his and bent over her saddlebags and gear. "I thought I should offer you some things to help you to safety. I can give you a knife." She removed a sheathed blade, a fierce little thing likely meant for throwing. "And here are a canteen, bandanna, socks—they are too large for me—and some cartridges."

"A lot of good cartridges do me with no weapon." He accepted the box just the same.

"Take mine." She offered him her long gun, a well-oiled Winchester she usually carried on her saddle.

Jesse took possession of the weapon. "You're giving me your gun?"

"Oui. Pierre will not give up easily. He is stubborn and prideful. You need to be vigilant. Even if you never see him again, this is dangerous country. I would hate for more harm to befall you."

Throat closed tight, Jesse nodded. What could he say? He'd been stripped of his pride, his security, and dignity, and now Lorraine offered him a chance to restore that. But it had been her fault in the first place.

As though hearing his thoughts, she cleared her throat and wrung her hands. "I owe you more, much more, for taking so much from you. Perhaps in the future..."—she met his gaze with tear-glistened eyes—"you can find it in your heart to forgive me."

Jesse captured one of her hands again. She startled, then allowed him to draw her closer, setting both her hands on his chest.

He ground his teeth, resisting the urge to promise to go with her. Denying the need to tip her face and place his lips upon ones that so often frowned and now begged for forgiveness. But such behavior would be unsuitable to their future and likely cause Lorraine to feel more confused, even weaker in a time when she so needed to be strong.

"If you wish to even the score, I ask only that my suffering has shown you the error of your lifestyle and motivates you to live differently." He tipped her chin up, but only to peer into her eyes. "Does it?"

"Yes, I see that I have been closed-minded, bitter, and very wrong. Will you forgive me?"

"I do." He kissed her knuckles, chastely and perhaps too quickly, for she hardly had time to open her eyes before he stepped away.

But then the mask was back, fierce and determined, yet shadowed with humility. "*Au revoir.*" She hefted her things and started toward the wagon with her typical long strides.

"Four weeks." He spoke, drawing her attention.

She paused and swiveled her head, her eyes shimmering brown beneath her Stetson. "*Pardon?*"

"Will you write me and tell me how you are doing? If you haven't found work, I might be able to help you find employment in California."

"How would I reach you?"

"Just address it to my name at Alexander Mining Company in Los Angeles."

She nodded, avoiding his gaze, then lifting her chin before turning with a sweep of her skirts to the wagon.

Chest hollow, he stood like granite. He should have said something better. Promised her something or pressured her more. They might never see one another again. If he'd met Lorraine under different circumstances, perhaps introduced by friends, or he might have seen her perform at the Sells Brothers Circus... Such thoughts were fanciful, wishful, and not connected to reality in the least. He'd never know what happened to her, as was best. Lorraine was in God's hands now —as she likely always had been. *If anything good comes from this hardship, Lord, let it be that Lorraine finds a new life.*

The wagon heading toward Ogden rolled into the shadowy land as the sun slipped below the horizon. Jesse climbed aboard the one going to Franklin.

CHAPTER 6

*H*e was going home, so why did he feel as though a swarm of bees buzzed in his chest? The old farmer who helped the train passengers set the brake on his buckboard wagon when they pulled into Franklin that night. Winchester in hand, Jesse alighted on the dusty street with a thud. The Mormon settlement rose around him, a quaint little town on the border. A large sandstone meeting house with a shingled roof stood in the town square, shadowed in the moonlight. The train depot sat on the edge of town.

The farmer who had given him a ride landed beside him. "No luggage?"

"No, sir. Thank you kindly for the ride."

The man shook his hand, glancing at the raw rope marks peeking from the edge of his sleeves. "Where you staying tonight, sonny?"

"I figured on inquiring at the mercantile." A gunshot sounded. Jesse slammed his rifle to his shoulder and scanned the area.

The old fella looked up from his worn hat and gave him a pat. "Some housewife probably caught a varmint trying to get into her cellar. You're a might jumpy. If I's to guess, I'd say you are running from trouble."

Cold sweat still coating his neck, Jesse stood up straight, though he sensed the bead of a rifle on his spine. Was it real, or was he just remembering the gun trained on him when Lorraine prodded him into the cave? Hands slick, he gripped the rifle harder. "Is there a sheriff in this town?"

"Yeah, right down the street a ways. I can take you there once I've got my horses situated in the barn."

"I would appreciate that. Thank you kindly."

The old man nodded. "Jacob Backster. You just wait right here."

"I'd like to help you with the horses." Jesse spoke as he followed him into the barn. There was quiet except for the grumble of a milk cow. Warm light from a lantern Mr. Backster hung on a nail chased away the shadows.

Being indoors, even in a barn, after the robbery and wilderness trek seemed strange. Was Lorraine's life always like that? What if she didn't seek honest work but returned to Emil? Would she ever know the peaceful, end-of-day chores, a hearty meal, and good company?

His thoughts still turned toward Lorraine when Mr. Backster led him down the quiet streets. He should have gone on with her. Stayed with her until she found a job. But that was outrageous. He hardly knew her, and besides, he needed to return to Pa and Aubrey. He sighed, his heart weighing heavy.

"You walk like a man carrying a heavy load." Mr. Backster ambled beside him, a pipe sticking out of the side of his mouth.

"I am finding, recently, I do not always know the right thing to do."

"This is a *recent* problem for you?"

Jesse gave a nod, and the old man laughed. Jesse grinned, though the humor struck him. Had he in the past been too certain, perhaps even arrogant, in thinking he always had the answer? After he'd failed Aubrey, he'd sworn he'd not hesitate to act if he believed something was wrong. Might he have been too confident in that respect?

They arrived at the sheriff's office, and Jesse bid Mr. Backster farewell. Inside the stone building, he sat before an oak table. Sheriff Bernard had a mustache with curved ends that reminded him of a long-horned bull. He stared with beady eyes, taking in Jesse's general state, which was lacking.

"What can I do for you, son?" he asked.

"I was kidnapped and need to connect with my family." Even as he spoke, Jesse's left heel tapped.

Sheriff Bernard's eyebrows shot up toward his broad-brimmed straw hat. "Well, I'm sorry to hear that. I can help you. Why don't you tell me what's happened?"

Jesse started at the beginning, when he'd escorted the wagonload of gold from the mine on Cariboo Mountain. Then the trek to Franklin and the train crash.

"And you mean to tell me these men disappeared after the wreck?"

"Yes, sir. One, Beau, suffered a head wound and he couldn't walk well. I saw him and Pierre ride away while we were putting out the fire."

"And what did you do then?"

"Came back here. I needed a telegram sent to my father, Titus Alexander, in California."

"Well, I can do that tomorrow morning when the office opens. You've become something of a celebrity, Mr. Alexander." As he rose, Sheriff Bernard settled a newspaper before him.

The headline announced Jesse's kidnapping by a female bandit and detailed his disappearance. Pulse thumping, Jesse consumed the words. "A guard died?"

"Sure did. Funny you didn't mention that."

"Because I didn't know. I got knocked out while the wagon was still rolling."

"The newspaper says that a woman held up the wagon and murdered a guard. The driver got a good look at her before he was knocked out."

Jesse kept reading, taking in the information. It couldn't be true. Lorraine hated killing. But then, she'd nearly shot him the same night of the bushwhack. If she had murdered the guard, could that grief have inspired her to live better?

"Did you see a female bandit, Mr. Alexander?" Bernard twirled his mustache.

Jesse's throat became dry. Any chance of helping Lorraine disintegrated. She was wrong in robbing the gold shipment and hurting the guards. She'd admitted so herself. So why was he protecting her now?

"Well?" The sheriff frowned, and Jesse found a few words.

"I told you, the men who took me used the names Beau and Pierre. There were also two American brothers by the name of Baker."

"Baker?" The sheriff startled. "Now them I know, but they usually rob banks and stages."

"They took my sister's camera and left the gang the morning after the robbery. The people who took me against my will and did this"—he pointed to his bruised face—"were not female."

The near truth still felt wrong. A wanted poster was tacked to the wall behind the sheriff. Bold letters read, *WOMAN WANTED FOR MURDER!*

If Lorraine was guilty, he was helping her get away with murder. But she couldn't have done something like this. It was impossible.

"You are avoiding the question. Was there a female outlaw?"

Diverting his attention from the wanted poster, Jesse faced the lawman. "Yes."

~

*B*athed and clean shaven with a fresh set of clothes, Jesse spent the night at the sheriff's house. Throughout the evening meal, his stomach soured and his pulse raced. Had he done the wrong thing, offering Sheriff Bernard the information he had? What would happen to Lorraine? A question made all the heavier with the sheriff's three pretty daughters peering at him. They were of marriageable ages and looked at him as though their pa had brought home a possible groom. Blessedly, their gracious mother had tended to him like a broody hen to a chick, showering him with kindness. The thought of being reuniting with Aubrey calmed his heart. He had said goodbye in March, and it was now nearing the end of May. Soon. He would make it home soon.

He stirred a cup of black coffee with a silver spoon, then dipped a shortbread cookie in. The mahogany table was surprising, as the sheriff lived in a humble stone house. But his wife had brought some fine furniture from back East. She and her daughters arranged themselves in a semicircle of chairs while a warm fire crackled in the hearth. Bernard read from a big black Bible, his voice drawling through the story of how Jacob wrestled with God.

Jesse flexed his wrists. He sensed that battle occasionally and also felt the loss, just like Jacob. Jesse lost in life, especially with Aubrey and possibly now Lorraine. Why was he complaining? After all, God had provided a way for him to escape capture and return to safety. He would send a telegram first thing tomorrow morning, and Pa would soon connect with him. He would be on his way to Aubrey then, but what about Lorraine? God's angel wounded Jacob. Did his hip go back into the socket, or was it a lifetime wound? If so, resetting the joint would have been extraordinarily painful.

"Well, that's it for tonight." Sheriff Bernard closed the Bible. "If you'll follow me..."

One of his daughters popped up like a compressed spring set free. "I can show Mr. Alexander to his room."

The elderly man rose with Jesse. "No need, my dear. I will see he reaches the spare room."

Jesse thanked his hostesses and bid them goodnight, then followed a hawkeyed Sheriff Bernard down the hallway. He didn't miss the warning in his eyes, though the protective father had nothing to worry about. While his daughters were pretty, none of them were Lorraine. Jesse nearly halted at the thought. Good heavens, he was doomed.

~

*J*esse sat upright as he jerked awake. Darkness washed away the crimson of the nightmare, the motionless figure on the cave floor disappearing. His neck was slick with sweat, and his chest ached as though he'd been holding his breath too long.

Lorraine...

The flashes of the nightmare returned. He shook his head, trying to clear the images.

"God. Please protect her!" He pressed a hand to his chest. Just a hint of light from the cracked door alleviated the darkness. He rolled over again, only to freeze. Cracked door? A prickle ran along his neck, and Jesse recoiled with a fist ready.

A dark figure towered over him, hand raised with something that the intruder arched downward.

Shifting his arm up, Jesse blocked the blow and delivered his own into the man's gut.

That was the last thing he remembered.

The next morning, he stared into another campfire with Pierre and Beau positioned on the opposite side. Dawn settled on the surrounding wilderness, the hills open to the wind. The ropes binding his wrists were tighter than ever. The taste of iron filled his mouth from when Pierre struck him. They'd caught him again. The Frenchmen conversed as though he wasn't present, speaking of their activity since the crash which included following him to Franklin and watching him enter the sheriff's home. Soon their conversation turned ahead, to the remainder of the journey.

"But Emil said he wanted Jesse alive." Beau frowned deeply, one of his arched eyebrows swollen and cut from Jesse's fist.

"Well, he would be easier to move dead." Pierre spit across the blaze at Jesse.

Pain shot through his lungs, and Jesse clenched his jaw.

"I don't like this job. Taking gold is one thing, but people..." Beau squatted before the fire, shaking his head in disapproval. "It is wrong. Lorraine was right about that."

"Lorraine will agree when we get to Salt Lake. Alexander deserves what he's got coming to him."

"Oui, but what if she's not there?"

"You think she won't see Emil this close to the anniversary?"

Beau's movements slowed, his gaze vague. The man looked defeated, to say the least. The hunch of his massive shoulders made him no less dangerous, even if he had a care for Lorraine. But what anniversary did the men refer to?

"Jesse, sit up." Beau came about and kicked his leg.

He didn't react until Pierre dug a stick out of the fire and jammed it into his bicep. Jesse shouted, but it was Beau who knocked it away.

Pierre glared at his friend, then rolled his eyes. "You spent too much time with that woman." He stood and dusted off his pants. "Good luck getting him moving without my help." He turned away to ready his horse, which was tied near Lorraine's black steed and one Jesse had never seen before. Beau's must have died in the crash.

Beau crouched, his balled fists pulling the leather gloves taut across thick knuckles. "Listen, Jesse. I might not stick you with coals, but I will beat you senseless if you don't get moving on your own. You don't have to be dead to be tied over a saddle."

"There is no other way you're moving me, Beau." No sooner had the words left his mouth than Beau hoisted him up by one arm. Jesse rammed him with a shoulder, but Beau recovered and struck his unprotected gut. Breath shot from him, and he tightened his muscles, ducking the next swing.

Beau corrected and brought an elbow down.

Jesse turned enough to avoid contact. Giving himself space, he jabbed the heel of his boot just above Beau's knee.

Beau shouted in pain, doubling over in the same instant.

Not allowing time for him to recover, Jesse thrust his knee into Beau's face. He stumbled to the side, holding his bloody nose.

Amid Jesse's thundering pulse, Pierre laughed. Jesse turned around, ready to take him on, too, but the long gun in Pierre's hands gave him pause. Just enough for Beau to slam into him from behind. With his hands still bound, he had no way to brace himself. Jesse landed in the dirt, the side of his skull slamming so hard that light, then black flashed before his eyes.

Pain exploded on the side of Jesse's head. Against the backdrop of a tangerine sky, Beau wielded a rifle—butt first.

Jesse was spinning, the pain a torment as sharp as a dagger's tip. The blackness ate him up, though his body told him he was still alive. His skull thudded as if it might burst. He opened his eyes and glimpsed the side of a horse underneath him, an empty stirrup swinging below.

"I told you, unconscious or dead. But you just had to fight." Beau wound a rope around his arms and then the belly of the horse. A man, presumably Pierre, held his feet and fed the rope on the opposite side of the horse over which Jesse lay. "You hardly fought the whole time Lorraine was with us, but now you go to war. You must really be sweet on her."

Ears ringing, Jesse squinted as the horse swayed and sunlight poured over the crest of a hill and into his eyes. "If you had any sense, you'd let me go. The law knows I was taken from the sheriff's home. You won't be able to move in this land without someone noticing now. A man strapped over a horse. You might as well write your confession now."

A shadow crossed Beau's face, and he looked at Pierre.

Hurting too much to continue to hold his head at an angle to see Beau's face, Jesse simply let himself hang upside down, eyes closed as consciousness ebbed. "Lorraine will hate you if any harm comes to me."

Beau's voice seemed distant. "Why's that?"

"Because she let him go!" Pierre threw his head back with a laugh, cursing Lorraine.

With his resolve stronger than ever, Jesse ground his aching teeth. *Lord, protect my mouth from uttering anything that might give her away, and give me strength to resist these men.* He wouldn't make the journey easy for them—that was for sure.

CHAPTER 7

The hospital in Ogden, Utah, was significantly cleaner than Lorraine had expected. She sat beside Madam Sinclair, the woman from the train wreck she'd aided. The pale woman smiled weakly while her two daughters told their father about the train crash. He had received word of the crash and come to Ogden, not leaving his wife's side since arriving. His travel had taken several days, and in the meantime, Lorraine had enjoyed the privilege of tending the girls at a local hotel per their mother's request. It was as though God had heard her conversation with Jesse about being a governess and was giving her a chance. Both girls were clean, with thick brown braids framing pretty rosy faces, as they clung to their father.

Madam Sinclair cleared her throat. "Mrs. Jones tells me you are looking for work as a governess."

Lorraine inclined her head and made every effort to dispense with her accent. "I am."

Monsieur Sinclair reached for his wife's hand. "We will be traveling home once my wife is better, but I'm afraid she won't be well enough to tend the girls."

Madam Sinclair shook her head. "I certainly will not. We were wondering if you, Lorraine, would travel with us and look after the children."

"I—yes, I am happy to help." She held her hand to her chest, hardly believing the opportunity.

"We are also looking for a governess for the girls. They are getting older now and need to begin studies. If all goes well on the trip, we would like you to consider taking a position as governess in our home."

Lorraine stared, then nodded slowly. "I would be honored." Was this really happening? Was God making this way for her to make a better life like Jesse wanted? Might she also make a positive difference in the girls' lives?

Monsieur Sinclair released a relieved-sounding sigh. "You are truly a blessing."

Lorraine opened her mouth, but no words came out. One of the girls let out a squeal. She hugged Lorraine, who hugged her back.

Maybe Jesse was right. Maybe she could find a new life. She'd have to write Beau in a few months to tell him she was safe. A letter to Emil was in order too. She'd figure something out, but first, she needed to see if she could be a good governess. Oh, she'd done her fair share of tending children in her youth. How fun it would be to wake up each day to teaching. She would have to work on her English so her own illiteracy did not inhibit her tutelage. She understood English just fine, but since she had refused to speak it, she would have to work harder now. It was a shame that she'd been so bitter over leaving France that she had stubbornly refused to use the language here. She'd even refused American foods. Doing so had seemed so important at the time, but now it seemed childish. There was still time to amend her mistakes. Maybe God had His hand on her, after all.

A half hour later, Lorraine left the hospital room, her cheeks aching from smiling. She studied her ruffled slate-gray skirt, blue calico blouse, and leather men's belt. Her Colt was back at the hotel room—maybe not the safest thing, but she didn't want to carry a gun while tending the girls. She would have to get new clothes and dress like a proper lady if she was going to be a governess. Madam Sinclair had said they would cover the cost of two suitable outfits from a local dress shop before they started the journey. The Sinclairs really wanted her to work for them and care for their dear daughters.

Of course, she'd not make it to Salt Lake to commemorate the fourth anniversary of the Bloody Week. She'd so hoped to see Emil and light a candle for her mother at least. May twenty-first through the twenty-eighth were hard days for her, and today was the twenty-fourth. She had already missed her meeting with Emil on the twenty-first, though that was more for her benefit than his.

Was it better to not commemorate the days and go on with her life? Was she dishonoring Maman's memory otherwise?

She rounded a corner in the hallway and collided into a man. "Excuse-moi."

"Lorraine?" Pierre stepped back, wearing clean clothes, a new hat, and with his mustache shaved to a thin line. The man changed the way he looked often to avoid being recognized. He looked from side to side. "What are you doing here?"

"That does not concern you. What are *you* doing here?"

"Getting medicine for Beau." He lowered his voice. "He's back at the hotel, healing up after that head wound."

Beau was still on the mend? It had been five days. He should be well. "How is he doing?"

He shrugged, his features hard. "Would be a sight better if he stayed still instead of looking for you. Why'd you run off, anyway?"

"Me run off? You and Beau left me and took my horse. What choice did I have?"

He grabbed her arm. "Lower your voice."

Lorraine jerked away. "Do not touch me."

"Fine, advertise that Beau and I are in town. There are wanted posters all over this place."

"You saw one of Beau's wanted posters?"

He nodded, then stuffed a bottle she'd not noticed before into his pocket. "I'll tell Beau you said goodbye." Pierre strode away, nodding politely to a nurse in the hallway. He even walked differently, shoulders hunched and hands in his pockets. Less conspicuous than his usual strut.

Lorraine skittered after him, right out the front door.

"What are you doing?" He barely glanced at her as he started down the boardwalk, past shops with horses tethered to hitching posts outside.

"I am going to see Beau." She took his arm, but Pierre shook her off.

"I don't want to draw attention to myself, and here you're walking around in a man's hat."

It was true, wearing her Stetson set her apart, but it was not as though she'd donned pants that morning. "Just lead the way to Beau." She dropped behind him, glancing admiringly at an assortment of hats in a shop window.

Pierre strode into a mercantile, and Lorraine followed. The scent of spices and freshly whittled wood permeated the air. A shopkeeper looked up from gifting a little girl a peppermint stick. Lorraine flashed him a smile to avoid being obvious, then perused the merchandise in time to see Pierre duck out a side door. He was trying to lose her.

She followed, sighted him in the alley, and then hurried after him through a door, down a hall, and into a crowded lobby.

Grinning, Pierre handed her a rifle, then turned. "Ladies and gentlemen, kindly raise your hands. We are robbing this bank." His English words registered a moment before a lady screamed. "Everyone over here." He gestured to one side of the room.

A few ladies dashed toward the main door, but a tall man locked it, then turned his masked face toward them. His familiar, dark eyes flashed with surprise upon meeting hers.

Beau! Pierre had his bandanna up around his nose now as well, but a fuming banker stared right at Lorraine. She hadn't donned a neckerchief that morning, not seeing a reason to wear one. Now her features were exposed for anyone to see, and she still held Pierre's rifle.

People huddled near the wall, ushered there by Beau, who did not look wounded in the slightest. He tossed her a bandanna. "Get out back."

Lorraine turned and ran.

She burst into an alleyway, heart ramming hard. After setting the gun against the wooden boards of the back wall, she tied the bandanna around her neck. After all, she would be even more conspicuous outside with a mask. Down the alley, a horse whinnied. It was her mare, Silvia.

Lorraine took up the rifle and jogged down to meet her. The black mare tossed her head excitedly, the stirrups on her saddle adjusted for someone with much longer legs than Lorraine's. Beau was still riding her horse. Why?

Laughter sounded down the alleyway, and Beau and Pierre spilled out into the shaded way. Pierre, of course, was grinning, while Beau looked around worriedly, his arms full of money bags.

He saw Lorraine and raced toward her. "What are you doing here?" He slung the bags, fastened together with a rope, over the horse's back while Pierre pulled himself into his saddle.

Shouts sounded from inside the building. Pierre's horse

kicked up dust, as he sped off. Beau mounted, then reached for her.

A shot sounded nearby, and something hot slammed into her arm. Lorraine gasped and stumbled to one side.

Beau shot back, smoke wafting from his revolver. A man fell from the rear steps of the bank, into the dirt.

Lorraine covered the wound on her upper arm, warm blood oozing from beneath her fingers.

Beau dropped back down beside her and hoisted her into the saddle. She clung to the horn as he mounted behind her and spurred his horse into a gallop.

~

*J*esse hung his head, suspended from the cabin wall by thick ropes, with all his body aching. Flashes of the past four days came to mind, fighting Pierre and gaining the upper hand, only to be set on by a second man. Lorraine's good friend Beau hadn't shown him much mercy. He'd slugged Jesse repeatedly until he fell, too weary to fight. Pierre had taken his swipes, too, jabbing a sharp boot heel into Jesse's lower back. It had taken much longer to travel. He'd fought every conscious mile until the men happened upon the abandoned hut. Surprisingly, they had tied him up and left.

He opened dry eyes, his head aching as it had that first night when he'd awakened to Lorraine and Pierre fighting. This time he was alone. Distant thunder rumbled. He felt the vibration in his legs. Hopefully, it would rain, the whole valley would flood, and he would drown to death. Better that than having to deal with Beau and Pierre again. *Lord, please lead Lorraine to safety. Restore Aubrey. Make Pa strong enough to deal with what is to come.*

Horses murmured outside, then an angry voice swore in

French. The men had returned, their horses' pounding hooves the thunder. Thank heaven, Lorraine was far away.

The door to the hut opened, having been lifted and set aside since there were no hinges. Pierre stood with sunlight streaming past jingling spurs, chaps, and a wide hat.

"We need to leave before they catch up!" Beau shouted from outside.

Pierre squatted before Jesse and slapped his face. "Wake up!"

Jesse bit into the bandanna that had been around his mouth for however long.

"Hurry up!" Beau's voice echoed as though from far away, then nearer. The thump of him landing in the dirt told Jesse he'd dismounted and would soon join his partner inside. Instead, he spoke more gently, likely to the horses, but did not enter the cabin.

"I've got a little surprise for you, Jesse Alexander." Pierre gripped his chin and jerked it up.

He squinted into the bright light coming through the doorway as a woman swept into view. Sunbeams hugged the full skirts and blue calico shirt, the familiar tan Stetson stopping his breath. Lorraine stood holding her arm, blood staining one sleeve.

She tilted her head to one side. "Pierre, we will have to leave now if we are to outrun the posse you have surely brought down upon us with your recklessness." Her voice was cold and angry. She turned with a fanning of skirts and slipped into the sunlight.

Not a comment about his battered state, though she'd defended him before. Why? Had she been in cahoots with the men all along?

Pierre sawed through Jesse's ropes, then when he fell, dragged him into a sitting position. "Things have changed, Alexander."

It had only been since the train wreck that Pierre referred to him by his surname, and there was always a certain hatred attached to it that he'd not noticed before.

Pierre sat down in front of him, as though speaking with a friend. "I realized some time ago that you weren't going to cooperate without Lorraine. Well, she's back, and with a bullet in her arm."

Gag removed, Jesse closed his mouth, his tongue sticking to the inside and his split lip swollen. His voice was mostly gone when he tried to speak. "You shot her."

"Nope. Happened in a bank robbery. Your girl, fool that she is, went in without a mask. In a skirt too." He laughed and shook his head. "Not gonna be hard to forget her. Helps that she's so pretty and French. Wait." He thumbed his chin. "She didn't actually say anything. Probably too surprised. I guess she wasn't expecting to help rob a bank today. 'Course, she wasn't much help. At least in the bank. I think she'll be a lot of help now. See, this is how it's going to work..."

Beau poked his head into the cabin. "Lorraine says it's time to go."

Pierre's congenial expression fell to one of rage, yet his voice was eerily calm when he answered Beau. "Be there in a second."

"Good. I got Jesse's horse ready." He disappeared again.

"You know, I met a soldier from your American Civil War. He got shot in the arm. The wound wasn't clean, and guess what happened? The arm was so infected, they had to cut it off at the shoulder. Right here." He made a slashing motion under his shoulder like a blade severing it. "Can you imagine Lorraine missing an arm?"

Jesse's already racing heart thundered. He was so angry, he felt ill.

"Her left arm too. That's her good shooting arm. I don't think Lorraine would be much good with only one arm. Maybe that could become part of her new act. You know she was part of a traveling show. That's how she does all the tricks. Losing her arm could make her life really hard. Poor woman." His expression turned stone cold. "Things will get a lot harder for her on the ride between here and Salt Lake City if you don't cooperate. A fall from her horse, riding too hard, or a bit too much of this..." He pulled a bottle labeled *Laudanum* from his pocket. "Beau and Lorraine wouldn't know what hit them. Just imagine having to watch her fade away, knowing you could have made her last few days of life easier."

"So you're set on killing her?"

"Whether or not she lives depends on you. I didn't shoot her after the train wreck when she let you go. In fact, I would've been happy never seeing the woman again, but you have made every moment from Franklin to Ogden miserable." He punched Jesse for good measure. "She wouldn't be here if you had just cooperated with me."

Head hanging, Jesse waited for the pain to recede. "Fine, I won't fight you, but we stop to take care of Lorraine's arm as soon as it's nightfall."

"As soon as it's safe, we will stop."

"How did you find her, anyway?"

"Beau just couldn't help himself. He had to know what had happened to her, so I seized the opportunity to get some leverage on you and gold in my pocket. Now, get up. I'm not waiting around here for a posse." Pierre pulled Jesse up and shoved him toward the door.

Outside, Lorraine sat astride. Her ruffled skirts spilled over the horse's side, stocking-clad calves showing just above a pair of ladies' boots. She clasped her arm, now tied with a bandanna.

Beau swung into the saddle behind her. He glared at Jesse, his large, muscular arms coming around Lorraine as though to claim what was his. Jesse's currently imprisoned brother-in-law had looked at him like that when Jesse and Aubrey spent time together. Was Beau protective? Or something else? Lorraine stared ahead, not looking at him.

Pierre took the lead, and Beau and Jesse followed. His head pounded out the recurring question...

Had she planned to meet with the rest of the gang all along?

CHAPTER 8

*D*arkness fell, yet still they rode. Jesse protested multiple times, and Pierre deferred to Beau as though he was in charge. Was he doing that to make the hotheaded man feel like he was in control?

Beau supported Lorraine, whose head lulled from side to side on occasion, the bandanna around her arm sopped through. Why was she so near slumber? She'd stood in the doorway of the shack with strong bearing. During the ride, she seemed nearly unconscious. Pierre must have already slipped her the laudanum.

Finally, they stopped in the woods at the base of a steep slope of the Rocky Mountains. The temperature had fallen surprisingly low.

Pierre dropped onto the forest floor and began kicking out an area clear of twigs and branches for them to set up camp. "I'll build a fire, Beau, if you want to take care of Lorraine." He ordered Jesse to sit beside a log, whispering another threat that if he ran away, Lorraine would lose her life. The man was so confident that he hadn't bothered tying Jesse the whole ride.

Beau might not want Lorraine harmed, but Pierre still

posed a danger. And Beau was a fool. Just because a man cared for someone didn't mean he had the heart to defend her or the wisdom to know when to do so.

Beau spoke softly to Lorraine, and she murmured a reply Jesse couldn't understand.

"What's wrong with her?" He tightened the muscles in his legs against the urge to stride across the clearing.

The man ignored him and lifted her down from the horse, only to lay her in the dirt.

"Beau, you risk infection by putting her on the ground when she has an open wound."

Beau's face turned red. He lifted Lorraine, only to stand there like a lost boy. Jesse unsaddled the horse and quickly made a bed of the blanket. Beau laid her there, then stood back, wiping his palms on his pants.

Jesse turned, jabbing him in the chest. "Why's she practically unconscious?"

Beau brushed him off and reached for Lorraine's bandage, only to grimace and pull back. He murmured something in French before wiping his sweaty forehead.

"You should wash before you touch her wound. She'll get gangrene and have her arm rot off if you don't."

As expected, Beau shuddered and drew away.

Pierre carried an armload of firewood into camp. "What is going on?"

Beau fumbled speechlessly, all the brute strength seeming to leave him.

"We need boiling water to clean Lorraine's wound, a needle, clean cloths too." Jesse turned to the men. "I can take care of it. I know something about dressings." He'd had to learn when Aubrey came home after an accident. Her selfish, arrogant husband had been drinking and ran their carriage off a bridge shortly after they were married. Of course, she had defended him. The memory sending a shudder through him, Jesse knelt before either man answered.

Beau unsaddled the horses and set up camp. He was like a different man with Lorraine back. He'd been more impulsive and mean when it was just him and Pierre. Might Lorraine be his anchor to decency? Or maybe Pierre brought out the worst in Beau. He was impressionable, as Lorraine had said.

Jesse arranged the things he'd need to bind Lorraine's arm, then waited for the kettle of water to boil. There were no other marks on her body, no bruising on her head to signal that she'd been knocked unconscious, but she didn't respond when he called her name. She wasn't feverish.

The men sat down by the fire, Pierre talking about a nearby settlement with a brothel. His crude remarks didn't seem to affect Beau, who glanced concernedly at Lorraine. They allowed Jesse to wash himself at a nearby stream.

When he again knelt beside Lorraine, he faced the men and put his hands on his hips. "I'll need a knife to cut away her sleeve."

"Not going to happen, Alexander." Pierre slurped a can of cold beans, smacking his lips as he wolfed down the contents.

"All this bloody fabric needs to be removed and the area around the wound cleaned. Do you want Lorraine to lose her arm?"

Beau whipped his head toward Pierre, who—staring forward—handed Jesse his knife as smoothly as if he was passing peas at the dinner table. As soon as he released the blade, he pulled his gun. "I might not be as fast as Lorraine, but I hit what I aim at."

Jesse nodded and turned to his work, a cold sweat breaking across his neck when he felt the gaze of the weapon yet again. He was tired of being powerless. Tired of worrying about Lorraine and those around him, especially Aubrey and Pa at home. *God, I've tried to get out of this fix alone. I can't do it.* He cut away the sleeve of Lorraine's shirt and peeled back her makeshift wrappings to assess the damage.

Please, provide a way for Lorraine and me to escape, and please heal this wound.

"Hand it back." Pierre interrupted his prayer, reaching out a hand expectantly for the knife.

At least he put away the pistol when Jesse gave it back.

Halfway through cleaning the wound, Beau headed into the woods and spilled his freshly eaten dinner. Pierre laughed and wolfed down the remainder of his. He obviously didn't mind the sight of blood.

Lorraine lay still, not even wincing even when he cleaned the wound with the contents of Pierre's flask.

"You drugged her, didn't you?" Jesse glared at Pierre while Beau was off washing his mouth out at the stream.

"Did I tell you where I found Lorraine?" Pierre looked up, rubbing his thumb across a minuscule mustache. "In a hospital. She was visiting some family, the Sinclairs, from the train crash. Seems they needed a French governess for their brats. Beau doesn't know it, but Lorraine was about to leave for good."

So she did want a better life. "How come she didn't leave with them?"

"Well, all I had to do was tell Lorraine that Beau was hurt, and she came running, right into the robbery. When poor Lorraine was hurting bad with that bullet wound, I slipped some of the laudanum in with her water. She probably never knew, and once she was drowsy, Beau kept giving her more as we rode along."

He rose, and Jesse instinctively moved in front of Lorraine, but Pierre simply stretched his arms high to the trees. "She's much better company unconscious. Of course, I didn't expect her to stay asleep this long. Beau," he yelled over his shoulder, "how much of that water did you give Lorraine?"

As though on cue, she brushed one of her fingers against the side of Jesse's hand. So she was conscious.

When Beau didn't answer, Pierre shrugged and headed for his horse. "Well, I'm not staying out here with you lousy oafs when there's better company to be had."

"You're leaving?" Beau returned, looking very pale.

"Oui. You want to tie up Alexander and come to Mary's with me?" Pierre worked his saddle into place. "You look like you need a drink."

"What about Lorraine?"

"You think she'd make better company?"

Beau startled, his eyes bulging and hand shifting back toward his gun.

Pierre, who was either stupid or brave, actually laughed. "Beau, I'm not serious. I know Lorraine is like a sister to you. Why do you think I was willing to let her go after the train wreck?"

"He is lying." Jesse closed his fists tight where he sat beside her. "Pierre does not care about you or Lorraine. He would shoot her in the back the first chance you weren't looking." Jesse glared at Beau, shaking his head. "Why do you follow this man? You know he put laudanum in Lorraine's canteen and now she won't wake up. You could have killed her."

Beau looked confused, yet turned to Pierre in question.

"He hates Lorraine. Whose idea was it to get Lorraine in Ogden when she could have been away from this life looking after little girls? Working a respectable job?"

Pierre laughed. Light shone on the tree trunks towering around him as he saddled his gelding. "Don't listen to him, Beau. He is just trying to trick you. If Alexander had his way, we would both be dead, and then he'd take Lorraine away."

Beau's shoulders rose and fell, a struggle seeming to work behind his dark eyes.

Pierre placed a hand on his shoulder, his motion brotherly

as though he was now stepping up to take back control since Beau had failed. "Tell you what, I'll help you tie him up, and we can go to the brothel. You've been playing the part of a good man for Lorraine's sake for too long. She'll never know you left, and you can have a bit of fun with a worldly woman. Lick your wounds, considering today is the twenty-fourth of May."

Beau's eyes went hazy, but when Pierre moved toward Jesse, he followed.

Jesse stood, fists up.

Pierre snickered. "Now, why fight us? You know we'll win in the end."

It was true. Jesse hated that, but even with the knowledge that Lorraine was awake and the hope that she could release him once the men went on their way, he couldn't stomach being bound again.

Beau swung out a right. Jesse dodged and backed away from Lorraine, dashing under Beau's arm in the process. The bigger man huffed and cursed.

Every time they'd met at fists, Jesse had fought him head on. He hadn't attempted to evade him the way he did now. After missing again, Beau huffed. Jesse dodged several blows. When Beau swung at Jesse and nearly fell over, Pierre laughed. Finally, the man drew his gun and pointed it at Lorraine. "All right. I'm ready to leave." His voice was ice cold.

"You won't kill her. You said yourself that you brought her back because I wouldn't cooperate. You thought if you had her here, I would willingly go to Salt Lake with you." Jesse had refused at the cabin and been beaten something terrible for it. Being strong was easier with Lorraine not there. No, it just took a different kind of strength to refuse to fight.

"So cooperate!" Pierre walked toward Lorraine.

Refusing to fight wasn't an option when she was debilitated by overdose. Jesse held his fists up to Beau, salty sweat dripping into his eyes.

When Pierre neared Lorraine's still form, Beau lowered his fists. "What are you doing?"

Pierre kicked Lorraine. Both Jesse and Beau shouted, but not Lorraine, though it must have taken great restraint on her part.

Beau was suddenly on Jesse, throwing him backward. Pierre grabbed him around the neck, and the two of them subdued him. Ropes once again cutting into his wrists, Jesse soon lay beside Lorraine, his face to the ground.

The men made quick work of saddling up their horses. Beau took time to glance at Lorraine. "Why is she still asleep?"

"Probably the laudanum." Pierre laughed at his expression of horror.

Beau backed away from Lorraine, wiping his hands on his pants and looking between Jesse and Pierre. "You mean, her water was drugged?"

"To help her rest." Pierre shrugged, but Beau covered his face as though to block out the world.

The man was a wreck. No anchor in life. Just drifting between anger and fear. What a dreadful way to live. Pa had been right when he said that a man's code of honor was what he relied on in life. Beau loved Lorraine but was weak. If Jesse had the opportunity to convince him, he might turn Beau against Pierre. As it were, he lay bound hand and foot, too sore to even shake his head.

Stumbling to his horse, Beau wiped his forehead and knocked his hat to the ground. He picked it up, then mounted and rode off to the brothel with Pierre.

After the tread of the horses faded into the night, Jesse raised his head where he lay an arm's length away from Lorraine, bleeding into the dirt. "Lorraine? They've gone."

She sat up and groaned. Teetering to one side, she steadied herself with her good arm. She blinked, her words slurred. "Jesse?"

"Yes, hurry. There should be an extra knife in Pierre's saddlebags."

"Jesse, I thought you got away." She reached toward him, only to fall forward. "You're hurt."

"Do not fret over me, Lorraine. Get the knife."

Forcing herself to her feet, she swayed before dropping to her knees. The effects of the laudanum must be especially strong. Lorraine half walked, half crawled to the things the men had left and searched through them. Jesse tried to direct her, but she seemed to struggle to see. Finally, she found the knife, and moaning in pain, she held her arm to her chest and made her way toward him. "I don't think I am steady enough to cut your bonds without severing a finger."

"Just start with those at my boots." The leather would protect him.

At last, the ropes were cut. Lorraine blinked hard before peering at the rope behind him. It was not without a lot of pauses and a nick or two that she freed him. Arms released, Jesse brought them around and rubbed his wrists, only to reach for Lorraine when she slumped to the side. She shook her head, likely fighting for consciousness.

"Come. There is one horse left. One they got after the wreck." He supported her weight, trying to pull her to stand.

"Go without me. I will slow you down. Besides, you should not be seen with me. I will draw the wrong kind of attention."

"What do you mean?" He settled her head in the crook of his arm.

Lorraine panted, her face very pale. "Pierre's pack. There is a poster."

A yellow piece of paper lay on the disarrayed belongings Lorraine had plundered. Stomach hot with dread, he gently laid her back against the saddle blanket, then went to Pierre's things. Shaking his head, he glanced over the same poster he'd seen in the sheriff's office in Franklin. "You are wanted for shooting a guard."

Lorraine tilted her head. "I didn't do it. Beau and I took the gold we stole to a nearby mine Emil uses as a front. Pierre or one of the Bakers must have killed the guard."

So that was what had happened to the Alexander Mining Company gold. He'd wondered why none of it was to be seen but had assumed Pierre had worked with an even larger gang. This was much worse. Not only had Lorraine disarmed him and the driver, but she'd also smuggled the gold away and was now wanted for murder.

"How did your face end up on a wanted poster?"

"I fought the driver. He must have identified me. Pierre said there were wanted posters in Ogden. He must have seen mine and hoped by leading me into the bank robbery, I would be identified. He always hated me, and since he could not win to my face, he stabbed me in the back. Just as you said he would."

Setting down the poster, he went to her, but Lorraine stayed him with a hand. "You need to leave. I didn't have on a mask today in the bank robbery. People will see the poster and recognize me. They will track me from the bushwack in Idaho."

"I'm not leaving you." Jesse swept his arms around her.

Wincing, she pushed against his chest. "I will just slow you down. Listen, Beau left my saddlebags over there. There is a secret pocket in the lining. Take the money there and ride home, to California."

He shook his head. "You want me to abandon you, likely to your death?" That he could not do.

CHAPTER 9

The woods around them like soldiers standing guard, Jesse prayed instead for angels, lest Pierre and Beau return. The lady in his arms seemed no nearer to escaping with him.

Lorraine lifted her face to the sky, tears falling in streams. "What irony that I should find my ruin this week."

Gut tight and arms trembling, Jesse clenched his fingers together. "What is significant about this week?"

"It is the four-year anniversary of the Bloody Week in Paris."

He asked what she surely wanted to share. "The Bloody Week?"

"Yes. The Germans occupied portions of France after the war. Paris was under siege. When they left, we had few more freedoms. The Commune revolted against the new French government, then military attacked the city for seven days. Hence, the Bloody Week. My cousin used petroleum to set military buildings on fire, as many of the women who supported the Commune did. The following day, our neighbor lady was seen with a similar bottle and shot on sight. No warning. I found her in the street." Her lower lip trembled. "It was just a bit of wine."

Hating the horror in her eyes, he scrambled mentally for something to contradict such a terrible truth. "Pierre said you were a Roma."

She sniffed, smiling a little. "My maman was a Romní, and my pere was a French military officer. When he died, she returned to her people and I with her."

"Was that when you were part of a circus?"

"No. I work for the Sells Brothers Circus now, but I had some experience performing from my Roma roots. We traveled the country and camped on the outskirts of Paris at times. No one wanted my people within, though they could come to the camps to see us perform. When I came to the age of needing school, she asked a friend of my father's to take me to a school for girls, the Château d'Écouen."

"My mother grew up in France. She attended that school as well. Your maman must have wanted you to be educated properly."

"Yes, properly, and the nuns of the *Congrégation de la Mère de Dieu* saw to that. I suppose they were harsher on me because of my Roma blood. They wanted to make us into modest mothers and wives for France."

"Where was your mother at this time?"

"With the troupe. I would return when I could, but with the civil unrest, it was difficult. She wanted me safe, in school."

"Why did you stay in Paris after school? Why not return to the troupe?"

She sighed long and stared into the fire. "You can't just move around the way you can here in America. We had been at war with Germany, so traveling wasn't always safe. Besides, my mother was hurt in an accident and was no longer able to travel with the troupe. It was her idea to live in Paris. I think she could have traveled, but she did not want me to fall in love with a Roma and live the life of a wanderer."

"I suppose Beau did not like that?"

"No, he is like a brother to me. As the only children of the troupe who were half Roma, we were often treated as outcasts. He wanted our children to play together beneath the wagons at supper times. To gather around the fires to hear tales in the cold evenings. He was married once and had a son." She sighed, and something in Jesse's chest relented. So she did not have a romantic history with Beau.

"I was able to work in Paris to support us with the help of other ladies. Many of them were lost during the Bloody Week. When the military gained control, they arrested anyone suspected of supporting the Commune. We were poor, and with my cousin being a *petroleuse*, an arsonist, we were arrested. I was so angry that they came into our home. I resisted and was struck several times. Maman tried to defend me. They shot her, because of me. We left her in the yard after being chased away like animals." She bit her finger, blinking as though to hold back tears. "I prayed that a kind neighbor would bury her, so I could go back and pay my respects, but many of the bodies were thrown into mass graves." This time Lorraine gave in to shiny tears that trailed from beneath her lashes, down her cheeks. She covered her face, as if to conceal the evidence of her suffering.

Unable to resist any longer, Jesse wrapped her in his arms. She leaned into him and there unleashed her sobs.

God, how can she survive such suffering? He caressed her hair away from her face, whispering prayers of hope and safety for her.

When at last the torrent ended, her voice was quiet. "Many, including myself, were rounded up on suspicion. We were held in prison. Those found guilty of revolt were sentenced to servitude at the penal colony of New Caledonia. The soldiers came to get them, and when they did, they took everyone. We were herded into trains like cattle, on our way to the coast where a ship would take us to Australia." A vagueness entered her eyes, numbness as though she were reciting something someone else experienced. "Some of my mother's people, including Beau, boarded the train and were able to rescue a few of the prisoners."

"And that is when you broke your arm?"

She nodded. "Beau had connected with Emil, who had immigrated to America. We lived in a French settlement back East, but Emil wanted to move westward. Beau was indebted to him. I didn't want to live even farther away from France or work in Emil's illegal business."

"You knew then he was a criminal?"

"If he hadn't been, I would not have left France alive. He smuggled me out. When the circus came through town, it was as though God answered my prayers. I knew the types of men they were, and I did not want a life of thievery. I only got involved after I believed they had a plan to help my people. The holdup when we took you was my first robbery."

"Why rob others when you have lost so much? Shouldn't you be all the more compassionate?"

She met his gaze, her coal-black eyelashes wet with tears. "My motives were not selfish. My people are still imprisoned for the uprising. My cut will be sent to them, to pay fines and free them. To support their families."

"But they were rebels."

Traces of dirt remained where her tears had washed away the grime of the day, and her brow hardened. "Wanting freedom from an oppressive government is not wrong. Did not your country start as citizens of England who rebelled? The Commune was not the answer, true, but what person when faced with the hope of a better life for themselves and their loved ones will not sacrifice all?"

He nodded, mesmerized by Lorraine, who was no longer filled with dullness and weariness, but with conviction and belief despite all she had suffered. Lorraine was so strong, not just in the muscles corded around her ribs or the solid thigh against his, but in her spirit. She'd suffered so much yet not broken.

"This is your anchor, what you fall back on when you don't know what to do." His voice halted when she pressed more securely against him.

"What is my anchor?"

"Your belief in your cause. Helping your people."

"Yes, my people are important to me, but I'm not certain my course of action was the best. You have suffered because of me. I was wrong." She looked to the side. "You must go, now. Leave me here—"

He angled his chin enough to reach her lips, stopping their movement for an instant by gently pressing his to hers. The soft meeting forced a blaze through his veins, though he knew better than to linger there. Head spinning, he withdrew. "You mustn't ever think of defeat. Keep fighting."

She fluttered her lashes, brow furrowed, then rested her head beneath his chin.

He was grateful she'd moved before he did something stupid, like kiss her again. What had come over him? He'd never kissed a woman without first asking to do so and only the few ladies he'd courted. He prided himself on being controlled, certain, and cautious.

Wishing to cup her jaw and bring her lips to his again—to kiss her for all her courage, pain, and utter loveliness—he held still. Surrendered to prayers that he hadn't the words to speak but all his soul prayed.

*S*omewhere in the darkness once they left camp, Lorraine found warmth and strength. Leaning in, she sensed a potential fall but trusted all would be well. When the horse they rode together shifted, Jesse's bearded chin nudged her eyebrow. Weariness carved lines in his features, but his darkly circled eyes met hers with calm. "Didn't think you'd awake."

He spoke French as clearly as though he'd been born in her land. His mother must have used the language often in his home. "I am very weary." All her body was weighty and terribly shaky. Spears of light wove through the horizon, contrasting the gray rocky hills. "Where are we going?"

"The next town."

"I told you to leave me behind." She let her eyelids fall.

"Not an option for me, Lorraine. I won't leave you again. Not after last time."

What an odd thing to say. "At least tell me you took the money from my bags."

He adjusted the blue bandanna she'd given him at the creek. "I did." He patted his shirt pocket. "I grabbed your saddlebags so we have a knife, your Winchester, and supplies."

"Good." She shivered and wiggled her cold toes, which tingled from how long her legs had dangled over the horse's side.

Jesse touched her forehead, his hand delightfully cool, and then urged the horse into a quicker pace.

"Where are we going?"

"The next town." His voice was taut. "Remember?"

Remember what? Stars dotting her vision, Lorraine tipped her head up. The sky stretched from north to south and east to west. Lovely. "But why are the stars still out when the sky is light?"

Jesse firmed his hold on her. "Stars? What else do you see?"

The day seemed to be growing dark. Was a storm on the horizon?

"Lorraine?"

My, he sounded alarmed. Perhaps there was a storm. That would account for him hurrying the poor horse.

CHAPTER 10

*S*alt Lake City nestled in a valley with the Wasatch Mountains rising to the east. The sparkling waters, after which the capital city of Utah was named, skirted the edge of the city. Farther to the west was another range of mountains.

Jesse cautiously maneuvered the horse on the road, a chilly wind rushing down the hill behind him and scattering the sandy soil. This was the last place he'd like to be, but the closest, and considering Lorrain's condition, the best option. He turned up his collar and held Lorraine a little closer, his arms aching from supporting her feverish body through the night. They needed to be careful, even here. While Salt Lake had an estimated population of around thirty thousand inhabitants, news of a man bringing a wounded woman into town would spread. The last thing he needed was his or Lorraine's whereabouts in the papers.

He nudged Lorraine awake, testing the temperature of her forehead again. Why hadn't he thought to grab more water when leaving Pierre and Beau's camp?

She startled and looked around, her breathing choppy.

Jesse lightly squeezed her. "Steady, Lorraine. You're safe."

Her dark-lashed eyes floated downward.

"Oh, no. Wake up. Sit up straight and listen to me."

Her cheeks were terribly hot to the touch, yet she'd not complained a peep over the last few hours of riding. "We have reached Salt Lake. I do not want to draw attention to you, but you're shot in the arm."

"What do you want me to do?"

He swallowed. Hopefully, the plan would work. "I want you to sit up straight. Behave as though you are well and not hurt. We'll check in as a married couple at the hotel, then I can call a doctor. Can you do that?"

"I will strive to do my best." She straightened and squared her shoulders.

After that, her body moved more succinctly with the horse's, which was good, except she must've been expending energy to do so.

Along the busy street, they passed many carriages and the railway cars that made their way down Main Street to Second South. The four-story Wasatch Hotel sat on the corner. Constructed of brick, the building stood with a level of renown that would hopefully keep away the likes of Pierre and Beau. Besides, it was within a block of the Western Union Telegraph office. He could send a messenger to the office to have another telegram sent to Pa. The sheriff in Franklin must have already sent one as well.

They passed into the shade of the porte cochere, and a porter ran out to meet them. He took one look at them—dirty, bruised, and travel weary—and squished up his face.

Jesse wasted no time swinging from the saddle. "Hello, there. My wife and I were just out for a ride when her horse spooked." He flipped two silver dollars into the air. "See this one to the stable while I get her settled. I will round up some gents to find the beast." He grinned and plunked the money into the bewildered kid's hand.

Jesse untied the saddlebags with their few supplies, then reached for Lorraine. She smiled and descended into his arms as though indeed a blushing bride. Despite her tight grip on his arm, she wobbled. He adjusted the coat around her to hide the fact that her arm was in a sling. Pushing worry aside, Jesse plastered on another smile. After that, the porter took the horse by the reins.

Inside the richly furnished lobby with large windows and comfortable seating, Jesse settled Lorraine in a cushioned chair. The money he'd taken from her saddlebags could rent a room, but he needed more for a doctor.

At the front desk stood a middle-aged lady with a high bun and equally high collar. She smiled with an all-business attitude. "Mrs. Schubert at your service. How may I help you?"

"Yes, ma'am. I need a room."

Her shrewd gaze scanned his face, no doubt wondering about the bruises and cuts.

"What will this cost me?" He raised his eyebrows with meaning, but her expression softened.

"The usual, a dollar-fifty a day. Room 28 is available. Please sign into our guest book."

Jesse did so, writing the last name Lorraine had told Mrs. Jones after the train crash. He did not include Lorraine's name, and Mrs. Schubert did not remark. "I will also need to send a telegram to the sheriff at Franklin."

"Just write the message, and I will have it off to the Western Union in no time at all." She pushed a piece of paper toward him.

Jesse scribbled a brief communication, requesting the local sheriff contact Titus Alexander regarding news of his son. Hopefully, that obscurity would be enough to protect him if the message was intercepted but communicate to Pa that he was needed in Salt Lake. Jesse folded the paper and gave it to the proprietress.

She scribbled the room number next to his name on the guest book. "Is there anything more?"

"Yes, ma'am. Could you send for a doctor and Marshal Morris?" Lord willing, the old fella would help him out. But how could he tell him of his predicament without giving away Lorraine? She was a criminal, but falsely accused of the murder. If the law discovered her, they might attempt to transfer her to the jail, where she would undoubtedly be at risk of dysentery and further infection. Telling law enforcement about Lorraine for now was not an option.

Mrs. Schubert took a room key from a cabinet and handed it to him. "If you wait in the lobby, I will send a maid with fresh washing water and to stoke the fire."

"I am capable of stoking the fire. If you could just send up the water, please." The lady gave him a nod, then Jesse helped Lorraine to their room.

When at last they reached the door in the dim inner hallway, her knees failed, and Jesse had to carry her over the threshold.

Settling her on the bed, he took a clean shirt from the saddlebags then, pulled up Lorraine's coat sleeve. The inside was caked with blood. His stomach twisted at the sight. No wonder she was so pale. He maneuvered her from the garment. Lorraine's eyes closed, and her breath caught, though she uttered no word of complaint. Next, he unwound the bandages to reveal her inflamed upper arm, swollen with that nasty hole oozing.

Someone gently rapped at the door. Jesse stilled. The Winchester was there beside the bed. Pierre and Beau couldn't have found him so quickly.

Another rapping sent him into action. The bed was within sight of the door. He couldn't open it with Lorraine in full view.

"I'm going to move you. No matter what you hear, Lorraine, you must remain still."

"Who's here?" She lifted her head, shaking with the effort.

Jesse eased her off the bed and onto the floor, kneeling beside her to set a pillow beneath her head.

The knocking turned more rapid, more demanding.

"I don't know, but I sent for a doctor. If something happens to me, Mrs. Schubert will see you're taken care of."

She reached for the gun, but Jesse signaled for her to be quiet. Lorraine panted, lips pale and eyes cracked.

What if she died? He gripped the rifle and crossed the room. Beau and Pierre wouldn't like what they found this time. In previous fights, he'd been unarmed. He wasn't leaving Lorraine again.

Plastering himself around the corner of the door, he turned the knob and allowed the heavy oak to swing open.

He waited, his thumb on the trigger, but nothing happened. "Who is it?"

Still nothing. Were they waiting outside, guns drawn? Ready to wallop him over the head and drag him to Emil?

Jesse cautiously peered around the corner, retracting his head to avoid potential gunfire. The way seemed clear. He moved to the doorway and checked the hall in a similar fashion. A maid was the only person there, walking away.

A maid. The wash water! Mrs. Schubert had said she'd send it up.

Jesse settled the rifle inside, then eased into the hall. "Excuse me, miss."

The maid turned, peering over a white pitcher with her large blue eyes. "Oh, hello, monsieur. I have your water." She rushed to him, blond curls bouncing with the youthfulness of a girl.

She must have assumed she had the wrong door when he didn't answer. "Yes, thank you. I will take it."

"Nonsense. I will set the room and stoke the fire."

He blocked her way, taking the pitcher from her hands. "I am capable. I appreciate the offer, though."

"Oh, is there nothing I can do for you?" She pouted, her French accent thick, though not as much as Lorraine's when she spoke his language.

"As a matter of fact, there is. A pitcher of tea and dinner, please." He found the required coins in his pocket, to which the girl curtsied deeply.

"Merci beaucoup. I am Marguerite, at your service."

"Thank you, Miss Marguerite." He nodded politely, then closed the door.

What a coincidence, running into another French woman out here in Salt Lake. He'd not met many who migrated to these parts.

Lorraine was awake when he went to the opposite side of the bed near the washstand. He quickly scrubbed his hands, then went to her side. He lifted her carefully, and once again, she uttered no sound.

"I never knew they made girls in France so tough." He untied the laces of her boots. "Must be your Roma blood."

That garnered the slightest of smiles from her.

"I will have to remove your dirty clothes. I've sent for a doctor."

"A doctor?"

"Yes, Lorraine. You need medical care." He slipped the second boot off her foot, leaving the stockings there. "I won't leave your side, though. You needn't worry." He reached for the collar of her shirt but stilled at the half-lidded gaze she settled on him.

"Did you telegraph your father yet?" Her voice was barely above a whisper.

How could she even think of that given her condition? He needed to get a doctor to remove the bullet and treat the wound before gangrene set in.

"Yes. Not that you should concern yourself with such matters."

She was quiet for several seconds, drifting off to sleep. Since she was still dressed in layers of ladies' garments, the fever would rage even more unless he loosened her clothes. He rubbed his hands on his pant legs. Lorraine was beautiful, and he'd struggled not to stare at her strong calves and delicate ankles when he'd found her at the stream after the crash. However, with infection taking hold, he experienced turmoil and something more profound—pain.

"Lor— Lorraine, may I remove your clothes?" Just saying it drove heat from his cheeks into his ears.

She lifted a hand, fingers fumbling with her top button.

He clasped her hand, barely breathing. "Allow me?"

Her consent, the slightest of nods, comforted him. He talked to her, explaining what he was doing and reassuring her she had nothing to fear. At last, she was resting in cotton under-things, her clothes in piles on the floor.

He drew a sheet across her body and set a wet cloth upon her forehead. Jesse carried a chair to her side and sat, holding her hand. The minutes dragged by, with Miss Marguerite bringing food and word that both the doctor and the marshal were away on business.

Jesse cleansed Lorraine's wound as best he could, then waited, praying and trying not to panic. Darkness came before the doctor's knock, and when Jesse rose to greet him, he prayed again, this time that the physician would not ask too many questions.

CHAPTER 11

The doctor closed his black medicine bag and frowned at Jesse. Lorraine lay on the bed, her cheeks bright red. Sweat glazed her forehead in the dim candlelight, while shadows crept from the corners of the room. Near the bed, in a dish of pink water, sat a little lead ball that the doctor had dug out of Lorraine's arm.

Had he been too late?

"Keep that fire low, just enough to keep the chill off." The doctor stood straight and tall beside the bed, his thick gray sideburns setting off sharp eyes. "If you think it gets too warm, open a window."

"Yes, sir," Jesse answered, as he had countless times since the old man entered the room and began his ministrations.

Now he gripped Jesse's shoulder. "I know you want answers, but I have none. Her body will fight the infection and win, or she will die."

Cold sank into his middle, and Jesse stood like granite. Even his thoughts paused in the face of such a threat. Finally, he managed words. "What can I do?"

"You can give her plenty of water, keep her cool, talk to her, and pray." He squeezed his shoulder. "Pray hard."

"Yes, sir. Thank you."

The doctor raised his eyebrows, and Jesse paid him the rest of his money. Though the old man said nothing, Jesse felt his disquiet. "Can you come by tomorrow?"

He started to shake his head.

"I should have more money by then, sir. I just don't want to leave her."

"It's not the money, son. I have others who need my assistance as well. Still, I will do my best to return if you so desire. However, you should understand there is little more I can do. Keep the wound clean and give her water. The rest is up to God."

Jesse nodded, and the old man left, bidding him farewell and closing the door quietly.

Jesse stood motionless, his booted feet staked on the rug. What was he supposed to do now? The spacious room contained a chest of drawers, a desk, bed, and sitting area near the fireplace, which currently held a mild flame. He carried a chair to the bedside and sat with his hands folded.

The clock on the mantel ticked while the fire crackled occasionally. Jesse leaned back in the chair. A circle of light shone on the ceiling where the shadow from the hurricane lamp settled. Was Pa gazing at a ceiling like this or out under the stars, searching for him? Hopefully, the sheriff at Franklin could connect with him.

"No! Stop! Please. Maman! Do not!" Lorraine's cry brought him from his pondering. She turned her head from side to side.

Jesse pulled the chair closer to the bed and took her hand. "Lorraine, it's all right. You are safe."

Still she cried. "No. I am sorry."

Fever-glazed eyes opened, and Lorraine raised her eyebrows. "Beau, is that you?"

Remembering some of what Lorraine had told him, Jesse held her hand more securely. "Oui. I came for you. All will be well."

"My arm." Her face twisted in pain.

"You broke it, silly girl. Jumping from the train."

"The train? Where are the others? Amelie and the others?"

"I didn't see them." What had Lorraine said that night about the train?

Beau and several Roms had boarded the train to rescue her. She'd not mentioned anyone else. They must not have escaped.

"Oh, no. They will go to New Caledonia." Her breath caught, tears rolling down her cheeks. "Why didn't you save them?"

What would Beau say? Had Lorraine posed that very question to him after the rescue? He recalled Beau looking concernedly between him and Pierre last night and found words he hoped would suffice. "I tried."

She averted her eyes and cried. Jesse knelt with his knees on the floor where he could more easily reach her. She leaned into him, and he pressed his cheek to hers, her subtle moan in his ear.

What a blessed life he'd had, experiencing the death of only one loved one. Not like Lorraine, whose mother had suffered at the hands of such terrible men. Aubrey's husband had hurt her, and Jesse suffered with her, but Lorraine had lost everyone. Where could she find hope amidst such grief? The answer came as quickly as the question had. "God will be with them and with you, Lorraine. You cannot bear the pain of the sin done against them. You know Jesus did that when He died on the cross." Had Christ also felt the pain of those who suffered, the way Lorraine did now? He'd never thought of that before.

Once her crying ceased, Lorraine let him give her a drink, then settled against the pillow. "I dreamed of this, I think."

Feeling the weight of such a statement, Jesse asked the same as he had in the cave. "Dreamed what?"

"Of giving up."

"You mustn't give up. Remember your plan to be a governess and live well?"

Her bottom lip quivering, she shook her head. "I missed my chance."

"Nonsense. That was one opportunity. I'm sure God will bring another if you have the courage to look."

"Jesse, without Beau and Emil, I have no one. I cannot even return to the Sells Brothers Circus. I'm tired of being alone."

He sighed, closing his eyes. How could he urge her to persevere for the sake of righteousness? Once again, Pa's words about having a code of honor to fall back on returned to him. What was Lorraine's code? Loyalty. And here he asked her to abandon her loyalties and start a new life. He ran a hand up her good arm and pressed his lips to her forehead. God would provide a way for her, wouldn't He?

She sighed, her warm breath fanning his collarbone, and Jesse grew still. Holding her, being so near her felt right, despite the circumstance. He'd never felt for anyone what he felt for Lorraine.

"You kissed me." Her quiet voice brought his eyes open to meet her gaze. "Didn't you?"

The memory warmed him as did the soft curve of her mouth now. The turn of her lips and gentle warmth in her eyes tugged at him. Lorraine tilted her chin ever so slightly. Heat in his chest tightened, and he lowered his head, his eyes closing in the same instant.

A knock sounded at the door. Jesse stilled, inches from kissing Lorraine.

Her brow furrowed as she looked away. "Who might that be?"

"I'll see." Jesse was half relieved for the interruption since he didn't have answers for Lorraine. He kissed her hand and promised to return soon.

Outside in the hall stood Marshal Morris. His long gray mustache hung loose on each side, and dust clung to his coat, chaps, and hat. He stuck out a hand as Jesse closed the door behind him. "What brings you to Salt Lake, Mr. Alexander?"

"Trouble. I got kidnapped in Idaho. I escaped and connected with a sheriff in Franklin, only to be taken again."

Marshal Morris raised wiry eyebrows until they furrowed against the brim of his hat. "Kidnapped?"

"Yes, sir. While I was guarding a shipment of gold from one of my father's mines."

"Aha. I heard about that, now come to think of it. Seems a woman was involved."

"It wasn't a single person who kidnapped me but a gang. There were four men. Two Americans, the Baker brothers, left the gang the morning after the robbery. The others were Frenchmen from Salt Lake. They brought me all the way here. I don't know for what."

"That is strange." The marshal pinched the end of his mustache, only to come away with a decent amount of dirt. He wiped it on his pants. "How's your sister doing?"

"As well as expected. She's back in California." The last place Jesse would want Aubrey was Salt Lake.

"So you're not here because of her?"

"No, sir." Jesse cocked his head to the side. "Why would I be?"

"Because her no-account husband up and died trying to escape."

The hairs on his arm stood on end. "At the penitentiary?"

"Yes, sir. About three weeks ago now. I was out hunting an escapee just today." He removed his hat and hit it against his leg, only to sneeze when a cloud of dust erupted. "You're not here for the will reading?"

"No, sir. I managed to escape about five miles outside the city. Figured I could come here and hide out until I contacted my father. I don't plan to leave until I've hired some men handy with guns. They'll not take me again."

"Reasonable." He inspected Jesse's face, then shook his head. "I sure am sorry you came into such a dangerous situation. I imagine your pa is hurting, both his children suffering the way you two have. Well, I reckon I can get home for dinner and a bath. I came straight from the trail when I heard you were in town, fearing you were out for vengeance."

"Vengeance? Against whom? Louis is dead."

"That is a fact. He had friends, though, and with his recent death, they have been plenty volatile. You just keep your head low. You hear?"

"Yes, sir. Nobody knows I'm here except you and the sheriff in Franklin."

"Fine. I'll swing by tomorrow and take your statement."

～

*H*e had already said no to housekeeping that morning, yet Marguerite persisted. Jesse frowned, rubbing the ache in his neck while the little blond French maid stood at the midpoint of the hall babbling about cleaning.

Miss Marguerite pressed a bucket against her starched black-and-white uniform. "All I ask is that if you leave, you let me know so I may fulfill my duties."

Her accent slipped, sounding more English. Or maybe she was growing more proficient in speaking. Should he worry she might be connected with Lorraine's boss here in Salt Lake?

"Well, monsieur?" She raised her eyebrows, all business and the silliness from earlier gone.

His cheeks warmed. Pa was better at putting his foot down.

"I have not left the room for personal reasons. I need not explain myself—"

"Oh, non. I meant no disrespect." She sighed and hung her head, shoulders stooped. "Madam Schubert wants the rooms cleaned. She makes me stay late. I have to go home to my maman before dark."

"I apologize for the inconvenience." Headache intensifying, Jesse scrubbed his face. "Rest assured that you needn't stay on my account. The room is fine. If you would just continue to bring food, that will suffice." He scraped the bottom of his pocket for a few coins and got the expected smile when he placed them in her palm.

"Very well, if you are sure. If you go out, you can leave me a note at the front desk."

Rather than ask why, he bid her goodbye. Thank heaven the woman stopped talking. He closed the door and returned to the chair he'd pulled up to the bed.

Sunlight swept through in strips of open light where the curtains parted, the occasional flutter from outside air causing the shadows on the rug to waver. There on the bed, Lorraine lay in utter stillness as she had for the last few hours—since he'd given her a spoonful of pain medicine.

Jesse sat with his elbows on his knees. He hated how still she became after taking the medicine. As though she were dead. He held her hand, finding comfort in the gentle throb of her pulse. Between the bouts of delirium, fighting off whatever haunted her, and her tears, he'd feared she would hurt herself. At least with the medicine she could rest.

Another thump sounded at the door. Jesse closed his eyes. Hopefully, it was not the maid again. She had been a tremendous help until she'd insisted she clean the room.

Instead of the woman, Jesse found Marshal Morris on the other side of the door.

"Good news," he started without greeting. "Your pa was in

Franklin when your telegram reached the sheriff there. He's coming this way. Sent a wire to the bank here about a loan, too, so you can get some money." He moved to come into the room, but Jesse blocked his way.

"That is great news." He stepped into the hall, Marshal Morris's frown signaling he noticed the odd behavior. "I want a cup of coffee. Will you join me in the restaurant?" Jesse fished the key from his pocket and locked the door so no one could enter while he was gone. Lorraine was sleeping peacefully. If he was going to leave, now was the time, though he was hardly presentable—as confirmed by Morris's glance at his unshaven face.

"Sure. It will do you good to get out of that room. We can eat in the kitchen so no one will see you." He gave Jesse a pat on the back. "I imagine this ordeal has been quite a trial. It will be over soon. You just tell me everything you know about that gang that took you."

Downstairs, the kitchen was piping hot. Mrs. Schubert asked no questions when the marshal requested they eat in the kitchen. She even excused the dish washers to take care of other duties so the men could talk. Jesse chose his words carefully in relaying the events that happened, starting with the robbery on the road from the mine. He provided as many details as possible, noting that he was knocked unconscious and describing how Pierre and Beau worked. The Baker brothers were more a side note, even though they'd stolen Aubrey's camera.

Nearly three months had passed since he stood in his study, challenging her to go abroad? Bragging that he could indeed capture the entirety of Grays Lake in a photograph? Would the camera make a difference to her if she was not ready to come out of her despair? Lorraine had wrestled with the trauma from the Bloody Week for four years. How much time might Aubrey need? What could he even do when he went home? If Lorraine was proved guilty of murder... His chest bound up at the thought. He would find a way to help Aubrey and save Lorraine. Somehow.

Where was Pa? He would know what to do.

The marshal twirled his long mustache, his brow wrinkled thoughtfully. "You know, the driver of the gold shipment that day said a woman knocked him unconscious. No one saw any other people. The sheriff in Franklin sent him a record of your interview. He will have apprised your father of the details."

"My father is investigating, then?"

"Yes, sir. Hired an investigator and offered a reward for any information regarding this mysterious woman. No telling where she is now, though."

Jesse swirled his coffee inside the clay mug. He'd always been a terrible liar. His decision to remain quiet on the matter made him squirm inside, but he would tell the marshal once Lorraine was awake. If he did so now, she would feel betrayed and be even less likely to help the law. As it was, the likelihood of Lorraine turning over the gang was slim. Still, he had to try.

"We have a very small French community here in Salt Lake." Morris slurped his coffee and grimaced before adding a generous amount of cream. "I will do some nosing around and see what I can find out. Your pa should be here sometime tomorrow."

Jesse sat up straighter, his chest lighter at the very idea of seeing Pa again. He was used to being away from him—after all, Pa had business ventures all over the country and Jesse was a grown man. But he'd never not had Pa there when he really needed him. Such as when Aubrey was gone or when Maman died. Why had Jesse forgotten that Pa also suffered? Still, in his own quiet way, Pa had always been near, staying home for three months after Aubrey returned from her rotten husband.

Some of these thoughts still plagued Jesse as he climbed the stairs, patting the two keys in his pocket. It had been

Marshal Morris's idea to take the spare behind the desk. The last thing Jesse needed was the overzealous maid going into his room when he wasn't there and finding Lorraine.

He turned the key in the lock with a satisfied twist and breathed a sigh at the clicking of metal that signaled he could freely enter. His eyes adjusted to the dimness. The air was fresh, the carpet soft beneath his booted feet. When he reached the bed, light played across Lorraine's face. Her face was thinner than he remembered, though he'd only been gone a short while. A shudder passed through him. Her cheeks were pale as the pillow behind her, and her chest still. Jesse held his breath, focusing on the ruffled cotton chemise. Why wasn't it moving?

"Lorraine?" He touched her face, only to snatch his hand back for how chilled her skin was. Was she dead? Frozen inside, he pulled himself from the depths of fear and settled his ear above her mouth and nose. With the gentle rushing of air, he closed his eyes and sank to the bed beside her. Still shaking, he covered his face and uttered a prayer of gratefulness, pleading that God would allow him to remain close to a healed and healthy Lorraine in the future.

By the time dusk settled upon the city, Marshal Morris came by to tell him that Pa was delayed in coming, but perhaps that was God's way of giving Lorraine more time to rest and Jesse more time to plan. His first task was to clean up, shave, and dress presentably. If Pa glimpsed him in the dirty mess he'd been in since being kidnapped, he would be even more furious. Jesse would present himself in his usual, clean attire and spare Pa any worry. He would also get items for Lorraine so that once she was well enough, she could appear as the proper lady he knew her to be. The woman he'd seen on the train—Lorraine clad in a blue gown with ruffled lace collar—had been lovely and proper. Nothing like the outlaw she could be. Hopefully, he would never see Outlaw Lorraine again.

CHAPTER 12

*L*orraine tucked a strand of nearly dry hair behind her
ear, the scent of rose oil permeating her senses. Mrs.
Shuber's footfalls faded down the hall outside after
the kind woman had assisted her with a bath, then into bed.
The doctor had been in just before, and somewhere in her
memory, between long snatches of sleep, she remembered Jesse
nearby. But where was he now?

Sunlight swept through the hotel window, bright beams
slicing through the lace curtain. Lorraine eased off the feather
mattress on shaky legs and managed to drag a chair to the
window. In the busy street below, ladies in plumaged hats and
fancy gentlemen rode in carriages. Beyond them, standing in
all their rugged grandeur, the Wasatch Mountains with granite
sides rose up like a giant wave about to roll over them.

A knock sounded at the door. Lorraine turned, her toes
pressing into the soft carpet. The door swung wide and in
walked Jesse. He was clean shaven, sporting shirt sleeves and a
light gray waistcoat that hugged his thin stomach. He stilled in
the doorway, one hand on the knob and the other with a pack-

age. Though across the room, his clear eyes shone as though he stood mere inches away.

With a memory of firelight, tears, and his strong arms around her, her chest bound up. Then his lips settled on hers. "Jesse, why are you here?"

He furrowed his brow, then swung the door closed and walked past the messy bed, the herbal scent of cedar and soap following him.

They were alone in the room, though memories told her it hadn't always been so. The doctor had come to inspect her arm while Jesse watched from the shadows. So much of her memory was skewed with pain and fever.

"I thought you might want a clean set of clothes." He set the package on the table. "The hotel owner's wife helped pick this stuff out."

Lorraine cradled her arm and settled into the chair she had earlier dragged from the bedside to the window. "Thank you."

Jesse rubbed his palms together. "May I sit with you?"

"Oui." She gestured to another wingback chair.

He moved it to the window and sat. After all that time she'd seen him in denim, gingham, and boots, he seemed just as comfortable in his suit. Lorraine smoothed her cotton wrapper, tucking her bare feet beneath her.

The silence stretched, Jesse shifting from time to time and Lorraine avoiding his gaze.

He leaned down in his usual fashion, elbows on his knees and hands linked. "Pierre said you tried to leave with the Sinclairs. That they offered you a job as a governess."

"Oui. I hope they found someone to travel with them. Mrs. Sinclair was still very weak. Why did you come to Salt Lake, of all places?"

"It was the next stop on the rail line, and I needed to get you to a doctor."

"I see." She leaned back in her chair, knocking her elbow in the process. Pain split up her arm like lightning, chasing a tremble through her.

"Your arm became infected. I assume it is very sore." Jesse watched her, concern lining his features.

"How long have we been here?"

There was another knock at the door.

Jesse rose to answer it, speaking over his shoulder as he did. "Three days. Your fever broke last night, though I suspect you are still in danger of infection."

A petite maid waited outside, holding a tray and greeting Jesse with an exaggerated French accent and bright smile. Was she faking the accent for some silly romantic reason or to try to entice Jesse? Lorraine gathered her hair—black as midnight compared to the maid's blond tresses—and ran her fingers through it, trying not to meet the woman's gaze. Did Jesse prefer blondes?

"Thank you." Jesse's tone was all business when he took the tray.

The maid batted her eyes, only to narrow them at the sight of Lorraine.

What was Jesse thinking, letting the woman see her? She was wanted for murder. Forcing an amiable smile—after all, who would expect an outlaw woman to be nice?—Lorraine glanced away as though uninterested.

At last, Jesse closed the door. "Marguerite has been very helpful."

"I imagine she has." She caught a tangle with her fingers and pulled. "It is just a shame she is so nosy. If she's seen my wanted poster, she'll be quick to hope it's me." Still the knot stuck, so Lorraine tugged until the strands broke free.

Jesse frowned.

She met his gaze, then looked away. "I need to leave Utah. We're still too close to Idaho where the posters were issued."

"Well, you can't leave today. You've not had time to

recover. That wanted poster isn't much to go on. It described you as a pistol-toting, pants-wearing female. They didn't note that you were French. Both the doctor and the proprietress heard you speaking in French when you were delirious. As long as you stay away from pants and guns, you should be fine. Coffee?" He placed a cup in front of her and lifted the pot.

"I was delirious?" Cold prickles scattered across her neck. What had she revealed? Much, judging by Jesse's expression.

Rather than respond, he offered the coffee again.

She accepted the drink and toast, though by the time they finished, she was nearly too tired to chew. As she leaned back in the large chair, her vision blurred, and warmth surrounded her. Her thoughts wandered back to the maid, so eager in front of Jesse. She readjusted her head. It was really none of her business.

After all, as she'd said at the creek when he tucked the wood rose behind her ear, a future was impossible. Even if he forgave her, his father wouldn't. He had been robbed and would certainly seek justice for the loss of money and Jesse's kidnapping. She was the only one identified in the robbery, which meant she would have to pay or run. They would lock her in prison to rot with the rats and suffer a cold, dank cell along with precious little food or privacy. She shivered, hugging herself.

Memories from her past crept in, sliding around her like a moldy blanket—foul and suffocating. The darkness drew closer, as did the flashes of horror. Thundering feet of civilians mingled in with the screams. *Maman!*

Warm, strong fingers slipped between hers, gently tugging her back to safety. Jesse knelt before her in the light of an open window, the clean scent of soap and cedar reminding her that she was indeed safe. "More bad dreams?"

"Oui, they come often when I close my eyes."

"I'm sorry." Still he held onto her, rubbing his thumb against hers.

"You are so compassionate when I don't deserve it. I have been bitter and resented your countrymen for their good fortune. I've been so lost. Regardless, I never should have robbed your father's mine. I did not know they meant to abduct you." She stood, pulling from his grasp, and Jesse rose with her. "I know it justifies nothing. I was wrong to take part in robbing you of your freedom."

"We already talked about this. In the end, you set me free and would have released me long before then had I earned your trust instead of attacking you that first night."

"Trust you never should have had to earn, were it even possible to do so."

He drew back his head, voice deepening. "You do not trust me even now?"

Her pulse raced at the thickening in his tone, the bob in his throat that signaled an anxious swallow.

"I do, oui." Lorraine cradled her hurt arm.

"Will you sit down with me?" He gestured to the chair, and once Lorraine was settled, he took his own seat. "I want to see you well, Lorraine, then I need information on your accomplices so I can get justice for my father and see that those who led you astray are put away."

"They did not lead me astray. I came of my own free will."

"What were you promised?"

She sank deeper into the chair, frowning. "Emil said a large percentage would go to those in New Caledonia. That he'd made a new contact and had a way to help them more than ever before."

"He's sent money to your people before?"

"Yes, some. But never so great an amount." Why not, though? They were his people too. He had the means to help them, so why had he not sent more?

133

"What did you do back East?"

"I worked for the Sells Brothers Circus. Trick riding."

"You are good on a horse. How did you get into the wagon when you stole the gold? You didn't jump, did you?"

A smile warmed her cheeks. "Oui. I can do that while shooting flaming arrows too."

"I would love to see that." Excitement nipped his voice, bringing the warmth of youth to his eyes.

"Come to the Sells Brothers and you will. The tour has already started, but I should be able to catch up once my arm is healed."

"You're returning to the circus? Why not work as a governess for the Sinclairs?"

"I disappeared after promising to go with them. They will not trust me again." Her stomach sank. It would have been nice to be a part of a family, at least in a small way. "Going back East would be better. Besides, they know me by a different name there."

His eyes widened. "You...Your name is not Lorraine Durand?"

"It is. I used a false name at the circus."

"Oh, good." He sighed.

Had it mattered to him to know her real name? The notion tipped an inner smile for the sweetness of it.

Jesse scooted to the edge of his chair, his attention wholly on her. "If you worked for a circus, how did you end up on Cariboo Mountain?"

"I was going to visit Emil for the anniversary of the Bloody Week. He said he wanted to do something big to honor those who had died and help those still alive, but he needed money. He needed gold. I got caught up in the grand idea."

"Understandable. If he did plan to kidnap me, he'd know you wouldn't go along with that, so he told Pierre. If that was the case, though, how would they even know I, the owner's son, was riding guard on the gold transfer?"

"Pierre was in the camp to scout out why the wagon was so late. Likely, he learned that the owner's son was riding shotgun and took the opportunity."

His expression darkened. "That makes more sense than Emil kidnapping me. Besides, how would he know I was there? Salt Lake is a long way from Cariboo." He brushed a finger below his bottom lip. "You said Emil used another mine near Cariboo Mountain to hide the gold?"

"Oui."

"Do you remember the name of the mine?"

"No, but the man we met had a scar on his lip. It looked as though it tore and had never been stitched."

"That's Abe Johnson." His eyes opened wide, then Jesse shook his head. "He is Pierre's connection? He's my pa's foreman. And his friend…or so we thought. Man, we've known him for years. I argued and tried to get Pa to have Abe manage the mine, not me, when he sent me to Cariboo. He's been with Pa since his first strike. I never thought…I bet he told Pierre who I was. Abe managed the mine before me. He didn't like giving up control when I arrived. I guess this was his way of taking care of the problem. " He frowned and shook his head. "I will send my pa a telegram."

"You haven't already?"

"I did as soon as we arrived here. Sent a messenger so I wouldn't have to leave you when your fever was so high. Once it broke, I went to get you some things." He motioned toward the bed. "But I wasn't gone long."

Was that an apology in his voice? Lorraine swallowed the sweet thrill of his caring. But Jesse went on in his practical manner.

"There must be a link between Pierre and Abe Johnson. I

hope it's just him that's crooked and not others who work for us."

"I hope so also." She sighed, sleepiness once again creeping up on her. "Did you have any other questions, Jesse?"

He pulled out a notepad and pencil stub. "If you can give me Emil's full name and his address, I can give it to the marshal."

"The marshal?" Lorraine sat up straighter. While Jesse forgave her, the law would not. "Have you been in contact with him already?"

"Yes. The same marshal who helped me last year when I came here for my sister," he answered measuredly. "You will need to talk to him and the police as well."

She stood up and headed for the door, expecting a pistol-toting, tin star–wearing behemoth to come barreling through.

"Wait, Lorraine." Jesse cut her off, using his body as a barrier to keep her from the door. "If you run, this will always be over your head. You need to face it."

"And be taken to jail? I think not." She went right and jabbed her good shoulder into his chest when he tried to stop her. The action was useless, since Jesse was as sturdy as a bear and the contact sent jarring pain through her extremities.

He reached for her arm. "As long as you cooperate—"

Lorraine back-stepped, one palm extended. "You want me to tell the authorities everything about Emil and his operation? Helping you is one thing, but talking to the law... The men who work for Emil are French. You expect me to betray my people?"

"They are criminals. Listen, I have a plan, but you need to do the right thing. I thought you were actually sorry." He pulled her away from the door with one hand on her waist and the other on her arm.

"I am, but that does not mean I will bring harm to my people. You do not understand. Emil saved my life. He was my father's friend. And Beau is like my brother. We were babes together, our mothers dearest friends. I cannot betray them. Let me go!" She turned and jabbed her elbow into his ribs, but he sat in the chair with his arms and legs wrapped around hers.

"Lorraine, stop. You will hurt yourself." Jesse held her gently.

The warmth from his skin infiltrated the barrier of fabric. She stopped struggling, her muscles trembling with fatigue. Gazing across her shoulder, she caught the alertness in his eyes as he looked down at her. He was so sincere and honest, she wanted to agree. Yet one thought made it through her foggy brain. "I want to do the right thing, but I'm not sure what that is. How can I betray my people?"

"You are not at war anymore. These men are not fighting for a cause. They are simply thieves, and if Emil wants to help the people of New Caledonia, there are legal ways to do that."

Lorraine shifted to see him better, his chest against her good shoulder. "What ways?"

"Raising awareness and funds. Writing letters to influential people. Sending missionaries. All ways to help, but you can't do any of that until you face this." His grip loosened around her, but Lorraine held to his arm, keeping it pressed to her waist. "I'll be with you the whole way."

"I am afraid." She barely kept a tremble from her voice.

"You think I would let anything happen to you, after everything we have been through?"

Unable to meet his gaze, she studied the cotton ruffles on her wrapper. "I-I don't know."

"Do you trust me?"

Lorraine nodded, his warmth enveloping her frayed nerves. She'd felt the tug of attraction between them before and resisted, but he was here now after sacrificing immeasurably to keep her safe. To stay by her side. "Jesse?" She ran her hand up his chest, not daring to touch the crevice at his collarbone. "You kissed me. Why?"

"It seemed right at the time. Under different circumstances..."

"There are no different circumstances. This is my life. Our relationship—set against impossible odds."

He breathed deep, fluttering her hair when he exhaled. "Nothing is impossible with God. I've never known anyone like you, Lorraine. You're perfect."

She snickered and touched the hollow at the base of his neck. "No one is perfect. Certainly not me."

"But you're perfect for me."

"Can such a thing be true, mon chéri?"

"I believe so." He drew her firmly against him. "*Mon amour?*"

She placed a palm on his cheek. "I'd hate for you to regret kissing me."

His eyelids lowered partway, his gaze on her mouth and voice scratchy. "Never." And he pressed his lips against hers in a firm but sweet seal of promise.

Sighing, Lorraine drew her arm around his neck to kiss him more deeply, even as reason cautioned against connecting with someone so dear yet so out of reach.

Jesse caressed her cheek, his movements tender—pausing as though to end the kiss, then continuing—until, with a groan of resignation, he met her gaze. "All that is pitted against us can be resolved if you are brave. Here's what I'm thinking... We can hire a lawyer, connect with the marshal who helped me rescue Aubrey. He will help you. And my pa is a merciful man. I know when he hears your story, especially about your time in Paris, he will forgive you."

"I fear you hope for too much." She smiled bitterly.

"You are innocent of the murder, and if you cooperate with the law, they will not seek to imprison you—a woman."

Lorraine tensed. He wanted her to turn herself in? What did that have to do with kissing? Resisting the pull of him and the fogginess in her head, she cleared her throat. "You trust your lawmen, but I do not. I've seen what governmental powers can do. How they prey on the weak. I am a foreigner in your land, at a disadvantage because I am poor and have no family."

"You have me, Lorraine." He cupped her cheek. "Even if you were not so lovely, even if I didn't feel as I do, I would be on your side because I am on the side of right. Talk to the police with me?"

"Can you promise they will not arrest me the moment I reveal my identity?"

Jesse grimaced. "No, but we can speak with a lawyer ahead of time." He kissed her forehead, leaving his lips there for an instant. "I will keep you safe. It's either this or run...run from me. Is that what you prefer?"

Lorraine shook her head, then rested it in the crook of his neck, soaking in his strength. How had she grown to feel so much for this man in such a short period of time? And what of his past? He'd said he failed to protect his sister. Did he need to make up for that by keeping Lorraine safe now? What would the Lord have her do in the end? Even if Jesse hired a lawyer, how would they prove she hadn't killed the guard?

~

*J*esse closed the door behind him, the shadows of the hallway crowding around him. He leaned against the wall, his Stetson in one hand. All those days with Lorraine fighting the fever while he was at her side praying, sorting his thoughts, making plans, yet he still wasn't sure what to do. He simply wasn't ready to say goodbye. "Lord, give me some direction here, please? What do You want?"

The shuffle of fabric and tread of footfalls sounded from

the other side of the door. Lorraine getting into bed, likely. She needed the rest. Or was she gathering her things to run?

His chest tightened, a warning soaring through him. If she ran, he'd never see her again. Might that be best since they still had no way to prove that she'd not killed the guard? He'd made a promise. He had told Lorraine nothing was impossible with God. Time to practice having faith. "You know I can't do this on my own, right, Lord?" He murmured the prayer and retrieved the key from his pocket, having left its twin on Lorraine's night-stand so she would not feel trapped when he secured the door from this side. Once Lorraine was safely locked on the other side, he pocketed the key and headed for the stairs.

In the lobby, sunlight poured through the multi-paned windows, setting shadows and light on furniture and a large oriental rug. The rugged mountainsides showed through the windows, rising up to snowy peaks.

Miss Marguerite met him at the bottom of the stairs, slightly out of breath. "Mr. Michel, how is your wife?"

The question jolted him. The marriage charade had been for Lorraine's protection, yet the notion appealed more than ever. A flicker of an image swept his imagination. Lorraine turning on her pillow, warm cheeks and dark hair. Lips rosier still as she reached for him.

Starved for air, Jesse pressed against his chest. "She is well. Thank you for asking."

"Oh, wonderful. You have a package." The maid handed him a flat parcel, about eighteen inches square.

"Was there a note with it?"

"No. I did not see who brought it. When I came back from running an errand, it was on the desk." Miss Marguerite clapped her hands as though his package was a surprise meant for her.

Jesse glanced around the lobby. There were people around

but no one who stood out to him. Who would leave him something? He didn't know anyone in Salt Lake except Marshal Morris, whom he had only spoken to briefly.

The maid still waited expectantly, so Jesse bid her farewell and walked to the kitchen where, at the request of the marshal, he'd been taking his meals in private. The room was empty this time of day. Once out of sight of the people there, he tore the paper to find a photograph. He froze as the tones of black and white revealed the face of a woman bound and gagged, looking at the camera with horror-filled eyes. Aubrey!

He turned over the photo to find scribbled words that stood out as clearly as though they'd been shouted into his ear.

Tell no one. Come alone.

Under that was an address and instructions to destroy the photograph. A cold sweat broke over his neck as his pulse pounded in his ears. Aubrey. He had to get to Aubrey.

Jesse took out his notepad and pencil, then scribbled down the address. He crumpled the photo and cast it into the stove.

Jesse stormed out the front door, waved down a public hack, and climbed in after telling the driver the address. The vehicle bounced along, and Jesse squeezed his hands together. Why did someone have Aubrey? He imagined her cries and shuddered. He needed a plan. To get to whoever was holding her and figure out what they wanted. Why hadn't the note asked for money?

He stilled. If they wanted money, they would have asked. They wanted him, and once they had him, there would be no reason to keep Aubrey alive.

He needed help. Marshal Morris would know what to do. Jesse pounded on the side of the carriage to get the driver's attention. The police station wasn't too far away from the hotel. But what about Lorraine? If they had found him at the hotel, surely, they knew she was there as well.

The carriage slowed to a stop. Before Jesse could lean out the window, the door opened and a man stepped inside. He seated himself across from Jesse, then removed his hat with a flourish. Pierre, smiling triumphantly, laughed and pointed a gun at his stomach.

CHAPTER 13

*L*orraine rolled over on the down mattress, bumping her arm in the process. She stilled, waiting for the pain to subside. Darkness filled the room save moonbeams slicing through parted curtains. How odd that Jesse hadn't come back. Perhaps he had returned and left while she slept. She certainly felt better with a cleared head and a less sore body.

Footsteps sounded in the hallway outside her door. Lorraine played with the end of her braid, waiting for them to pass. Jesse would never return to her bedroom so late. He was too proper for that.

The footfalls paused outside her door. Lorraine froze as a key scratched inside the lock. Why would Jesse come to her room in the middle of the night? Had something happened?

The door creaked open. A man crept into the room, his build strong yet with movements shiftier than those of Jesse's. Lorraine reached out to the nightstand for something, anything she might use as a weapon.

"Lorrie?" Beau raised his hands, outlined against the curtain. "Don't shoot."

"Beau?" She released a breath and swung her feet out of bed on the side opposite him, though she did not feel sturdy enough to stand. "What are you doing here?"

"I came to check on you."

"You drugged me, then ran off to a brothel with Pierre, and you want to check on me now?"

All was quiet, then his intake of breath signaled his stress. "You know I don't frequent brothels. I just couldn't bear to stay there with you like that...unconscious. I didn't know Pierre put laudanum in your canteen when I gave you a drink. I never—"

"And what did you do when you found out?"

"Jesse said he would take care of you. You might have been dead for all I knew. I couldn't take that. Couldn't bear to know." He rubbed his face, his breath coming faster. "I'm sorry. So sorry I failed you."

Remembering his tormented cry the night she was rescued and forced to tell him what had happened to his wife and young son, Lorraine drew in a calming breath. The last thing she wanted was to further hurt his scarred heart.

"I didn't know what to do. You were shot and had been unconscious so long. I was afraid..." His voice filled with emotions that extinguished Lorraine's ire.

On one hand, her heart broke for him. On the other, she pitied him. Why couldn't Beau be stronger, wiser, like Jesse? It was an evil, selfish thought, but as she stood before her lifelong friend, the difference between a wise man and a foolish one frightened her. And she would only ever trust one.

"None of that matters now." He took a step forward, desperation in his voice. "Lorrie, you're wanted for murder. Emil won't protect you. Pierre told him you let Jesse go. He's angry."

So they didn't know where Jesse was? She tapped her teeth together.

"We have to leave Salt Lake. I can take you back East. If you lay low, use a fake name, find another job, maybe you'll be safe."

"I can't leave." Jesse was counting on her to talk to his marshal friend. They were supposed to figure out the truth about the murdered guard and who worked with the kidnappers to steal Jesse away. No matter how hopeless the situation, she had to try. "I am still angry with you, Beau. How could you be so stupid? Why would you listen to Pierre when you know he is mean and dishonest? Besides, he has always set himself against me."

"You ran off, didn't even try to find me. What was I supposed to do? Pierre was the only person left. He is smart. Smarter than this stupid gypsy."

She winced at the crass term. "Nonsense. You know the difference between right and wrong. That makes you a hundred times more intelligent than him. You just have to hold on to what is right."

"I don't always know what is right." He shrugged.

"I know." She sighed and, shaking her head, lit the lamp on the bedside table. As the light flooded the room, Beau winced, then went to her side. Lorraine settled the glass shade onto its base and faced her friend. "How did you find out that I was here?"

"The maid, Marguerite, saw you—a beautiful woman with black hair, who also had a wounded arm." He gently squeezed her hand. "I knew it had to be you."

The maid had also seen Jesse. Beau was handsome and could charm the venom from a viper. "Beau, where did you get a key to my room?" The one Jesse gave her was still on the bedside table.

"The maid gave me one." He raised his eyebrows innocently.

"There were only two keys. I had one and Jesse had one."

Red infused his cheeks. "Jesse had a key to your room? You

145

just decided to take up with him, that stuck-up, rich American?"

"We kidnapped him, abused him, and hurt him, yet you criticize him."

"You ran away with him. Someone you hardly know. I thought we were friends, but you let him go after all the work I put into this job."

"I do not regret what I did. It was the right thing to do, and see how Jesse has proven himself to be honorable. He brought me to safety and paid for medical treatment when he could have turned me over to the law."

Beau shook his head, his jaw flexing.

"I never wanted a life of thievery. I only came on this job because Emil promised to send the money to help free those in New Caledonia." Her friend looked away, and something cold settled inside Lorraine. Why did she feel like a child, not included in a secret? Judging by his expression, an ugly secret. "Beau, the people in New Caledonia..."

"We tried to help them in the beginning, but there was no way."

"What?"

"I am sorry. It's true. Emil had no contacts there—any alive, anyway. Getting help for them is impossible."

Tears burning, she hugged herself. "That can't be true. I've been sending Emil money to give to them for years."

Beau collapsed into a chair, the same one Jesse had sat in earlier that day. "There is no way, Lorraine. Nothing we can do. I'm sorry."

She believed him. Beau had lost loved ones as well. Pressing her fingers to her trembling lips, she fought against tears. How could she have believed that Emil was so powerful, that his reach spanned the ocean? That the French government would allow him or anyone else involved in the Commune to help?

He had seemed like such a hero to her when she came to

America, still numb with the pain of losing Maman and the massacres in France. When he said they would help others, he'd given her a reason to live again. Lorraine stabilized herself against the side of the bed. All this time, she had been living in freedom in America, thinking that she was making a difference —that robbing others was justified. Her entire existence was a failure, and Jesse was in harm's way because of her. She had to free him once and for all, no matter the cost.

Lorraine took a handkerchief from the nightstand and cleared away her tears. "What happened to Jesse? I know you have his key."

Beau still sat with his head in his hands, though he gave her his shadowy, bloodshot gaze. "You hardly know this man, not a gentleman or soldier, not even French, and you love him."

"I feel something for him. If not love, something of the same vein. If there is any chance we have a future, I will fight for that."

"So you do love him?"

Looking down, she skimmed her fingers across her skirt. "I have only known him for two weeks." Still, he studied her, and another warning stole through her. "Why do you ask?"

He shrugged.

"Beau, you didn't get that key from the maid. You got it from Jesse, didn't you?"

His expression hardened.

"Did Pierre take him? You have to tell me now. Listen, there is something going on with Jesse's dad and their mine. Pierre's contact was a foreman of Alexander Mining Company."

"No, Lorraine, that's not true."

"It is! Pierre is fooling you and you don't even know it. Kidnapping Jesse has nothing to do with Emil or—"

"If that were true, why did Pierre keep him alive? Why bring him to Utah when it would be easier to send a ransom note from Idaho?"

"I kept him alive. He is an innocent man and doesn't deserve any of this. He even helped you when the train crashed." Lorraine headed for the door, nightgown and all.

"Listen to me." Beau caught her back by the arm, his grip lacking Jesse's carefulness. "Jesse may be good as you say, but it doesn't matter. He has blood on his hands."

Pulse pounding in her ears, she tried to pull away. "What do you mean?"

"He sent a Frenchman to jail. That man suffered in a prison labor camp—just like the people in New Caledonia. Jesse is an enemy to our people."

"That makes no sense at all. Jesse has nothing to do with the unrest in France and would never send someone to jail without cause. He is a good, honest man."

"You *must* love him to believe so easily." Beau released her arm. "Well, I'm sorry for that, because it's too late. Emil's got him."

Her body grew cold, and Lorraine stepped away from Beau and his terrible claims.

"Jesse *is* an enemy of the French people. He wrongly imprisoned one of our own. Emil wants justice. He'll do anything to get it. When Pierre said you set Jesse free, he was so angry that if you had been there, he would have killed you."

"Why? Did he know the Frenchman?"

Face growing high in color, Beau gestured with his hands. "That shouldn't matter. Foreigners are preyed on in this land, have fewer rights, and are easily set up by those who have been here longer. Who know the right people."

She inhaled deeply, grasping for calm in a sea of questions. "You are wrong. Jesse is innocent. Emil has the wrong man."

Shaking his head, Beau shrugged. "How can you be so sure?"

"If he was evil, he never would have helped you when the train crashed. Remember?" She wasn't going to mention his kindness toward her, which Beau would brush off as behavior driven by desire. "There has to be something we can do. Jesse said he knows a marshal here in town."

"Did you forget that we are both wanted? I won't give up my freedom for a fool who, even if he is innocent, is not one of my people."

"But what if Emil is wrong?"

"Who are you going to believe, some American who's got your heartstrings or Emil, the man who saved your life? Emil is a Frenchman. One of our people. If for no other reason, that is enough for me."

"It's not for me. Do you care nothing for what is right?"

"As far as I'm concerned, French is the right side."

Loyalty to his people. Preferring them and their rights to those of an American's, regardless of justice. Beau wasn't going to help her. She was lucky he wasn't turning her over to Emil.

Lorraine set one hand on her hip. "Where did they take Jesse?"

Beau shook his head slowly. "I'm not telling you just to have you try to rescue him and get yourself shot. You are no good to anyone dead, Lorraine. Least of all, Jesse Alexander."

"Fine. I'll figure it out on my own."

She turned and began going through the chest of drawers which Jesse had been kind enough to fill with her things. There were the fancy day dresses, but she needed something else to wear. She and Jesse had left camp with very little, but in the bottom of a drawer, mixed in with the frilly dresses he'd purchased at the store, were her saddlebags. In them she found her blue calico blouse, leather belt, and slate-gray skirt. Her boots were under the bed. What a shame she did not have her Colt, but she'd left it at the hotel room in Ogden where she had tended the Sinclair girls. Jesse had placed the rifle near her side of the bed. She could get it once Beau left.

Beau followed her around the room with a volley of questions. None of them mattered. She would not give up on Jesse, no matter what it cost.

Finally, her friend stomped off, cursing her for her "stupidity."

Lorraine dressed, then sneaked down to the barn just in time to glimpse him enter the street on horseback. In the barn, a number of horses were in stalls for the night, but one stood apart with a saddle in place. Silvia, her black coat making her nearly invisible in the dark. Her familiar neigh sent a thrill through Lorraine. Beau had left her horse for her, knowing she would follow. Was he setting a trap for her?

Unwilling to let him ride away when he was her only link to Jesse, she mounted Silvia and followed him into the night.

~

The streets of Salt Lake ended, and a cold wind rushed down from the mountain peak to the narrowing dirt road. Lorraine held the reins in her uninjured hand as her mare's hooves scraped on the rocky soil. Up ahead, tree branches settled shadows upon the moonlit gray land. Beau had ridden up into the hills on a dirt path, then veered off to a house that reminded her of old châteaus in the French countryside. Was this Emil's home?

Always, Emil had come to see her at the circus on special occasions such as the anniversary of the Bloody Week, her father's birthday, or even Christmas. Being separated from his father and stepmother who lived in what was now Germany, he must be lonely. She had never come so far west to visit him and would not have, had he not asked for her help in the Idaho gold robbery.

When had the man she'd once admired turned into such a calculating villain? Certainly, stealing a human's freedom had been villainous. And then Beau said Emil would have killed her when he heard she let Jesse go.

She obviously did not know him very well, a realization that saddened her already heavy heart. Her people in New Caledonia were as bad off as ever, Beau was not a good friend, and she did not even know Emil.

She reined in, her sore arm aching from the ride. Beau disappeared into the shadows of a barn. The moon slid behind black clouds, and a wolf howled in the distance. Lorraine's horse shifted nervously and turned its ears back. While not flighty, the mare had a certain uneasiness about her. If the beast spooked, she would alert others to their location. Might the animal smell the blood from Lorraine's wounded arm? The wolves would catch the scent as well.

"Do hurry, Beau." Lorraine hunched down, stroking the mare's neck.

When Beau reemerged from the barn, a lantern glowed from the back door of the château. There in the light were the unmistakable twin figures of the Baker brothers.

What were they doing here? After running off on Pierre, would not their returning to Emil hold punishment for them? Unless Pierre had told them to leave simply to stir up discord because of Lorraine's objections to the kidnapping.

Ye thought evil against me, but God meant it unto good. The Bible verse in her memory brought comfort. She huddled near a tree as she had the night she'd nearly killed Jesse. In that moment, she'd realized how much she needed God. "Thank you, God, for looking out for me even when I didn't deserve it." She kept her voice as a whisper while Beau and the Bakers stood talking.

The brothers headed for the barn, and Pierre and Emil took their places in the doorway. Pierre stood with a wide stance and puffed out chest. Emil, blonde and formidable-looking and with his shirt sleeves rolled up, apron over his front, sharpened a knife.

A question sounded in Emil's tone, though Lorraine could not decipher the words. Beau buried his hands into his side pockets, reminding her of the days when he wore short pants and ran barefoot near the streams upon whose banks they made camp. Would he give her away now, as a grown man?

A chilling gust stung her eyes, forcing tears, but even without the breeze, she could not stop the sting. Another lonely howl sounded, and Silvia stirred, tossing her head and making a fuss.

It was Beau who looked her way, glancing over his hunched shoulder.

She stayed still, hoping the shadowy trees cloaked her. Would he disclose her location? Had this been his intention all along, to entrap her and turn her over to Emil?

When the men turned away, he did not follow but instead, he went to the barn, where the Bakers had gone. Lorraine wheeled her mount toward town and rode as quickly as her injured arm would allow. Too soon she realized she had no idea what she was going to do to help Jesse.

CHAPTER 14

*T*his, of all solutions, really was the worst, but it was the only one. Lorraine lifted her hand to knock on the police station door which had a lantern burning on one side. A man's shout from inside stopped her. There was a familiar thrum in that deep male tone. Who was on the other side?

Footfalls thundered near the door seconds before it swung open. A tall man in a black hat shot out, knocking into her. He caught Lorraine by the hand before she could fall. With creases of age at the corners of his green eyes, though his hair was still quite dark, his features were hidden within the shadow of his hat.

"What in tarnation, Titus?" A middle-aged man with a brown bushy beard strutted through the doorway. He took one look at Lorraine and removed his hat. "Hello, miss. I am Chief Burt. What can I do for you?"

Lorraine blinked. "I need to speak with a federal marshal, Mr. Morris."

An elderly man who had been lingering behind the group in the doorway of the police station approached. "I'm Marshal

Morris." His gray mustache connected with wild nose hair. This was the man Jesse trusted so much? Surely not.

Chief Burt and the dark stranger strode past her, whatever tiff they were having carrying on with the officer's loud warning of caution.

Lorraine stepped nearer the entrance, preferring the mild mannered marshal. "I am here to report a kidnapping." How could she do this without having to give a long explanation and invite the marshal to lock her up? "A friend of mine was kidnapped by two men."

"Oh?" Marshal Morris's eyebrows curved low.

"Yes, my friend Jesse Alexander is from California. He said if anything happened to him to tell you."

Marshal Morris shouted after the big man who had nearly trampled her. "Whoa, Alexander. Get back here. I got news on your son."

Alexander? Lorraine's pulse thundered as the familiarity of voice and face struck like hot coals. This man must be Jesse's father.

Mr. Alexander turned from a huge black gelding. The light from the porch revealed his canvas pants, black leather chaps, and leather vest. A red tie knotted at his throat, a matching handkerchief sticking from his pocket. Jesse must have inherited his deep-blue eyes from his mother, for Monsieur Titus Alexander had keen green eyes that flashed warning.

"My son?" His inquiry was more a growl. "How do you know my son?"

Her throat dry, Lorraine swallowed. She stuck her thumb in her belt so her wounded arm—which was throbbing painfully —would not hang loose. "I met him briefly at the hotel. I am a maid there. He asked for both copies of his keys so that no one would get to him. We chatted over coffee." The lie spilled out, and Lorraine hated it, but admitting her real connection to Jesse would see her imprisoned and slow down his rescue.

"The men who took him," Chief Burt cut in. "What did they look like?"

"One was slender, shorter than Jesse with a thin black mustache and scrawny as a rooster. His name is Pierre Martin." She rubbed her temples, her head aching from the accusation and trying to speak English. "The other has fair hair, blond and gray, in his forties He walks like a soldier. I know the house they took him to. I followed them. I will show you." She nodded and gestured the men toward the street.

A tall man rode up on a horse. The tin star on his chest caught the light coming from the lanterns, as did his greasy nose when he pointed it at her. He reined in and dismounted at the hitching rail.

"Deputy Andrew, this young lady says she has news on the Alexander robbery and kidnapping case." The chief ran his fingers over the bullets in his gun belt. "We were just about to gather some men and ride out."

"We can ride to the location with this girl while you round them up. They brought Jesse all this way. There is no telling how big this gang is." Monsieur Alexander rolled his shoulders. "What do you say, Morris?"

Andrew jaunted up the steps, flicking his eyebrows at Lorraine. "Sounds good, boss. Let's get some rifles and head out."

The inside of the police station was warm like the gentle light of a kerosene lamp glowing from the desk. In the corner was a cot. A doorway led to the back.

"Weapons are back here." Andrew bumped into Lorraine's wounded arm when he passed, and her vision flashed as pain racked her body.

For an instant, the men's voices faded. She gritted her teeth, stifling a cry in her throat. At last, it relented when the front door snapped shut. Loraine opened her eyes, her vision foggy as she struggled to bring the room into focus.

Andrew stood with one hand still outstretched, having pushed the door closed.

Monsieur Alexander, Chief Burt, and Marshal Morris were peering up from a piece of paper. A wanted poster. *Her* wanted poster.

"And didn't we just get a telegram stating the gal in the Ogden bank robbery was shot in the arm?" Andrew charged across the room, grabbed her arm, and yanked her forward.

Lorraine shouted in pain and swung her good arm around and slapped him.

Just as quickly, his palm careened off her cheek, whipping her face to the side.

A man shouted.

Lorraine pulled back, fighting with her fists and feet. Finally, she broke free and stumbled back toward the dark doorway.

Blood drained from the sneering deputy's nose while the chief huffed. "Deputy Andrew, that is not how we handle suspects in my department—female or not."

Jesse's father puffed beet-red cheeks as he held a hand out toward the deputy, keeping him back, though he aimed a question at Lorraine. "Where is my son?"

Holding her arm, Lorraine panted. She had to get out of the small room before the men captured her. Her breathing hitched, then stopped as though someone had placed a hand over her mouth. Her pulse raced faster, filling her ears so loudly that the English words were lost to her. She struggled for air. Holding her wounded arm, she backed against the wall and shook her head. Slowly, she sank down, the men looming over her like a pack of wolves circling.

Deputy Andrew stepped nearer, his brows drawn so low, they blocked her view of his pupils. "You are the bandit-chit who held up the Alexander gold shipment and murdered a guard."

Monsieur Alexander pushed Andrew to the side. "Where is my son?"

"You're better off cooperating with us, girl." Marshal Morris bent over her, talking to her as if she were a child.

Only then did Lorraine realize she was on the floor. "I followed one of the men who took him to a house outside town as I told you."

Deputy Andrew scoffed. "We can't believe anything she says. She's a criminal, one of the gang that kidnapped the Alexander heir. Have you checked her for a ransom note?"

The two elderly men glanced at one another, but it was the chief and deputy who dragged her from the floor. No matter how she fought, they were too strong.

"Now, hold on a minute, miss. If you have a note, just give it up." Police Chief Burt held her arm, his grip painful, though nothing compared to the way Andrew squeezed.

"Really, men, must you handle her so roughly?" That was Jesse's father. His face was still high in color, and he reached out as though to interfere.

"I have no note!" She shouted in French. "Stupid soldiers. I came to help Jesse, and now you waste time." Loraine turned to the side, aiming her plea at Monsieur Alexander. "Your wife was French. Jesse told me. He is a good man and was taken by my boss, Emil—"

Andrew twisted her arm, and Lorraine went to the floor with a cry.

"Andrew, that's enough." Chief Burt pushed his deputy backward. "Go outside. You need to settle down."

Lorraine sat on the floor, covered in sweat, her vision blurring with the memories of the cells in the garrison in France where she'd been held. She could not find a way to escape. Her nose stung with the stench of unwashed bodies, blood, and death. French soldiers stood high above her, hauling out prisoners. Their screams filled Lorraine's ears.

"No...no..." She couldn't fade into those old memories now. She had something to do. Something important.

"Mademoiselle?" Monsieur Alexander's voice came through the darkness, like a lifeline on a black sea. He appeared above her, concern lacing his features.

Her fingernails scratched the wooden floorboards. Warm wood, because the day in Utah had been a hot one. She was in America, not France. The air in her nose smelled of gun oil and sweet tobacco. The marshal must chew the stuff. She was here, now, and wasn't giving up on rescuing Jesse.

A firm hand closed around her good arm. Lorraine jerked away only to find Monsieur Alexander kneeling in front of her, his expression calm. "That's enough, girl. You are safe now." He spoke in French, and suddenly, the world came crashing back into place. He, like his son, would not permit anyone to harm her. And the chief had backed his violent deputy up to the door, threatening to throw him outside.

"We must help Jesse."

Jesse's father offered her a large hand. "Quite right, and we do not have all night. I need your assistance. Will you help me?"

Lorraine nodded and allowed him to raise her on her shaky limbs. Once seated in a chair, she held her arm which was now bleeding through her shirt. She glared at Andrew and spoke between clenched teeth. "I have seen your kind before, filthy vermin." She spat at him, garnering a frown from the chief.

Monsieur Alexander, though, who was pouring her a cup of coffee, didn't seem to care.

Sipping the bitter drink he handed her, Lorraine tried to calm her body and collect her thoughts. "I am the woman you say I am." She met Monsieur Alexander's gaze but couldn't hold it. "I robbed your business and—"

"Hey, now, missy, you gotta speak English." Chief Burt stepped forward, pulling up a chair.

Monsieur Alexander scooted a chair beside her. "French or not, you should think about how much you want to say, sharing everything without a guarantee—"

"What are you, a lawyer?" The chief held up a staying hand. "Let the woman speak."

Monsieur Alexander stood. "My son—"

But Lorraine interrupted him. "Jesse is in danger. I know the house he may be at, but we have to leave now."

"We can't just blindly follow you into what might be a trap," Marshal Morris said.

"It's not. I can give you a confession once Jesse is safe. The man I work for is named Emil Jacques. I met him in France before the Franco-Prussian War. His name then was Emil Willot."

Monsieur Alexander raised his eyebrows. "Willot?" Alarm rang through his voice, and he snapped his gaze to Marshal Morris.

The lawman shook his head. "Willot died in the penitentiary this spring. It can't be him."

"Then some relation." He turned back to Lorraine. "Tell me, did he have any family here in America?"

"Not that I know of." It would seem Emil had been up to all kinds of trouble that had nothing to do with her. "Last Jesse and I spoke, we were trying to link Emil to your family. I didn't mention his given name, though."

"Oh, we are linked." Monsieur Alexander's knuckles popped as he clenched his fists. "My daughter married a Willot."

CHAPTER 15

*J*esse pounded his fists on the wooden door, with no returning answer. Darkness, deeper than what he'd experienced in the cave outside Soda Springs, closed in around him. He rested his forehead on the door and tried to think. Pierre had taken him to a house on the outskirts of town, a modest French-looking château, which Jesse soon learned had a decent-sized wine cellar. And here he waited, trapped again.

Footsteps sounded outside, coming closer. At last. Feeling his way, he moved away from the door. The scrape of metal on wood sounded, then light spilled into the room.

Jesse squinted, only to find a woman thrust into his arms. He caught her. She lifted her face, and her dark-brown hair fell back. "Aubrey!" He hugged her tightly, thanking God, yet nervous because he'd expected Lorraine. Lord willing, Lorraine was fast asleep and would not wake until tomorrow morning when, hopefully, all this was over.

"Jess, why are you here?" She looked up, tears falling.

"Move back." A man with a heavy French accent pointed a gun at them.

Aubrey gasped and scurried to the back of the cellar. Jesse stationed himself in front of her.

"You don't have long." He hung a lantern on a hook, then slammed the door.

Jesse turned to his sister. "Aubrey, are you all right?"

"I'm fine, I suppose." She spoke quietly, her large eyes shifting as though the dangers lay in the shadows. "How did you get here, Jess?"

"It's a long story." His own eyes adjusting to the light, he took in his surroundings. Wooden beams supported the ceiling, and wines and pickled items like olives and onions filled shelves lining the walls.

Aubrey sat on a barrel. Safe for now, and he'd need to keep her that way. His sister was different. Alert, awake, and—

Her hands rested on top of a large belly.

His cheeks heated as he pointed at her middle. "You're with child?"

"Yes, Jess. Now stop staring at me, for pity's sake. This is bad enough without you judging me." She lifted her trembling chin and glared.

"Judging you? Why would I do that? You are married. I'm just surprised. Louis..."

"Has been imprisoned for six months. The babe is his." She shielded her middle protectively.

"I didn't know you were with child. I'm sorry." His cheeks burned as he stood like an oaf, trying not to let his jaw hang loose. "Are you happy?"

A smile pushed up her cheeks, and some of his tension washed away.

"Good. Now, we just have to figure out a way to escape. How did you get to Salt Lake?"

Her shoulders slumped, reminding him of when she was a girl. "This is all my fault. Louis wrote to me from prison once I moved home with you and Pa. I told the maid not to tell you because I knew it would upset you. At first, I burned the letters unread, but after you and Pa left for the mines, I was so lonely, I started reading them. He said he was sorry. That he came to know God and was a changed man."

"And you believed him?" Jesse shook his head. "Surely, you are not that foolish after everything he's done."

"I am not foolish at all, Jesse Mark Alexander. I thought the least I could do was tell him about his babe. We wrote back and forth. The letters stopped for two weeks in the beginning of May, then a couple of days ago, he wrote me, asking me to visit him in prison. He said that he'd had his lawyer draw up a contract to give me and the baby a stipend."

"From what money? That which he embezzled and stole? Is that why we are here, Aubrey? Because your rotten husband tricked you?"

"Stop talking to me that way." Aubrey stood and crossed her arms. "I have no idea why you are here. I was taken off the train as soon as I arrived in Salt Lake."

"You came here willingly, after what Louis did to you? Did you forget what he did to your last pregnancy?"

Aubrey gasped and covered her belly, as though to shield the little one within from hearing. "That is none of your business. I wish you didn't even know. I came to sign paperwork to provide for my child."

"Why would you do that when Pa provides for you?" Jesse glanced around for something he could use as a weapon. He found a few long pieces of wood that would serve as clubs. They looked as though they'd been part of the shelves. Best to hide them. He stationed them at different locations in the room.

Why was Aubrey so quiet?

He turned to find his older yet petite sister standing with her hands on her hips, glaring through tears. "Because I was foolish! Because I wanted to hear Louis apologize for what he did to me. Because I needed to feel as though I mattered and what happened mattered. Besides, Pa hated Louis. Why would he tolerate his baby?"

Jesse sighed. "Because it is your baby, Aubrey, and you matter a great deal to us."

She rushed across the room into his arms, and Jesse hugged her even as his mind worked. "What day did you get the last letter from Louis?"

"He sent me a telegram on May twenty-fifth." Aubrey looked up, wiping away tears and glancing worriedly at their surroundings.

"That is the day after I escaped."

"So you were kidnapped as Pa said. If you escaped, what are you doing here?" she asked.

There was no sense in telling her about the photograph and note stating he should come here. That he had been free and safe and would have remained so if she'd stayed home.

"Everyone makes mistakes." He wound an arm around her.

So Louis had written her before he died. Should he tell her now that her husband was dead? If Aubrey did love him, might that send her into another dark mood like the one that had lasted for the months following her return home?

Jesse rubbed her back. "Did you tell Louis in your letters that I was at Cariboo Mountain?"

"Yes." Aubrey bowed her head and nodded. "I thought he was in prison. How could he get to you from prison?"

The bar on the other side of the door shuddered, and a thud followed. The door swung open, and in stepped a man with graying blond hair and familiar features.

Muscles constricting up his back, Jesse instinctively moved in front of Aubrey. While not his criminal brother-in-law, this fellow certainly resembled Louis—or rather, what Louis might look like in twenty years. All this time, Jesse had believed he had been kidnapped for monetary reasons. With the death of his brother-in-law and resemblance of this man, he had to guess the reasons behind the kidnapping were more personal.

The man stood with feet apart and arms crossed, a Napoleon of sorts, only far taller than the famous French emperor. He must be Emil. Behind him, the spindly legged Pierre closed the door, his usual smirk in place. Both men crowded the area. Neither were visibly armed, but that didn't mean they still couldn't overpower him and get to Aubrey.

Aubrey looked between the two men, the grooves in her forehead deepening when she focused on the blonde, yet she turned a questioning gaze to Jesse. He shook his head slightly. Hopefully, she would not feel as though she needed to take the lead as the older sibling.

The man who looked like Louis pulled up a crate and sat down, stretching out his legs as he surveyed the ceiling. "I love being underground. When I was a boy, we lived in the province of Lorraine in a house with a cellar." His eyebrows flicked up, and Jesse's pulse thrummed more quickly. "Yes, Lorraine. Like the girl who took you. Such a shame she was not more like her father. More French." He sighed, then reached for a jar of pickled onions off a shelf and pried it open.

Aubrey tightened her fists, her expression hard when she stepped forward. "Why did you bring us here?"

"Shut up, woman. We are here because of you." The man stood as though to stride across the room.

Jesse darted in front of his sister. "How do you know Lorraine? You were friends with her father?"

Blue eyes so closely resembling those of Louis slid to the side to meet his gaze. Jesse clenched his fists.

A knock sounded on the door. Pierre answered, though he didn't leave the room. His hushed words were too quiet to understand. Who else might come through that door? Likely not an ally who could help them. He'd not contacted Marshal Morris, and Pa didn't know where he was.

"Emil?" Pierre ducked back in and frowned at Jesse.

So he *was* Emil—Lorraine's boss and the man who had ordered his kidnapping.

"Speak." Emil returned to his pickled onions.

"The guard you set at the road just reported that Beau was followed here. By a woman."

Jesse stifled a groan. The last thing he wanted was Lorraine getting hurt. And, of course, she'd come alone.

Emil groaned. "I'd hoped she would stay away."

Pierre spoke with the man on the other side of the door, then to his boss. "Andre followed her back into town." He raised his eyebrows as though in question, and Emil nodded. Pierre and the man outside traded places.

This guard was significantly larger than Pierre, his arms like barrels. He had mentioned the name of an accomplice—Andre —so Pierre must not be too worried about Jesse or Aubrey telling the law.

Emil turned to Jesse. "What am I to do? This is a family matter. My family."

"Is Lorraine a part of your family?" Jesse scooted Aubrey onto a barrel and took one of his own.

"Her father was like a brother to me, but he was killed in battle. I swore to look in on Lorraine and her Romní mother. Lorraine, named after the birthplace of her father and myself, was like family to me." His gaze went vague, lingering on Aubrey for a moment, then he looked away, shaking his head. "I saw that she received a French education."

It was no wonder turning Emil over to the law was so hard for Lorraine. Jesse had been a fool to expect so much from her after all she'd lost. But why was Aubrey here? Weary of the conversation, Jesse tapped his foot. "So what is your connection to Louis?"

"My father married a second time, late in life. Louis was born from that union just six years before Lorraine. I sent him to America when hostilities between France and Germany began. I only wish I could have sent Lorraine away as well, but Paris was too far for me to reach with the German occupation."

"She said you saved her after the Bloody Week."

Emil shifted his jaw to one side. "She told you much. It's true, I was able to help a band of Roma put together by Monsieur Beau Fox. I should have known better than to call her in for this job. She is too softhearted for such work and too clever to fool. Yes, I saved her. A pity we saved so few. But you wouldn't understand that, would you—American? You whose father fought his own countrymen to free the slaves."

"Some people fight for others' freedom, not just their own. I might remind you that France has had a history of civil unrest."

Emil nodded resignedly. "I thought I was saving my brother's life when I sent him to America. He had gone to university, something I—a soldier—never had. He could have worked back East in New York City at one of the banks, but no. He chased adventure on the wild frontier. This is where your family comes into the picture."

Jesse dug his fingernails into the soft pine that was his seat. Aubrey sat beside him, so stiff he couldn't detect her breathing.

"You turned Louis in to the police. It is your fault he was arrested, and now"—he pointed his finger at Jesse—"my brother is dead."

Aubrey gasped and covered her mouth with one hand, the other flying to her belly.

"Good." Emil pointed to her, then smacked the guard's arm. "See, my brother's widow."

"No." Aubrey stood unsteadily, the baby obviously throwing off her balance. "That cannot be true. I wrote Louis and told him about the baby."

"Your letters were with his things from the prison. That is how I knew about my niece or nephew."

Aubrey shielded her belly, a feeble attempt, really, since her thin arms did little to cover the area.

"That is how you knew I would be at Cariboo Mine." Jesse crossed his arms as though he had nothing to fear. "So you want Aubrey's baby and my life. Then, three days ago, Pierre and Beau rode into town with news that Lorraine and I escaped. So you sent a telegram to Aubrey, pretending to be Louis. You figured I would go straight home, and then you could send a ransom note there."

Emil sipped from the jar.

"So how did you know I was staying at the hotel?"

The Frenchman smirked. "A little bird named Marguerite recognized Lorraine."

Jesse winced as though struck.

"Ah, you didn't know it was your fault, did you? You exposed Lorraine to Marguerite and she, being a competing, comparing, jealous female, was all too eager to find that the black-haired lady was indeed the outlaw I was looking for."

It was his fault. Lorraine had warned him about Marguerite, but he'd brushed aside her worry. Where was Lorraine now? Asking Emil of her whereabouts would be useless. The man would just as easily lie to him. Better to shift the conversation back into his control. "So your brother was a crook and died in prison, and you need someone to blame?"

Emil's nostrils flared.

"Well, Emil, or whatever your name is, here I am. How much investigating did you do? More than just Aubrey's letters, I hope."

Square jaw grinding, Emil nodded once, then threw the glass jar of onions at Jesse.

He blocked, and it shattered on the floor, spraying vinegar water in every direction. With the sour smell lacing the air, Emil darted forward, grasping for Jesse's collar.

Jesse lifted both arms, catching Emil's and pushing them

out before the man could hit him. Jesse punched him in the jaw. Emil fell back onto the floor, giving Jesse a moment to push Aubrey farther into the cellar. She hobbled back, cradling her belly and shouting over her shoulder that she would pray for his victory.

The little Holy Roller.

Jesse was ready for the guard too. The bulky man gripped a knife and came in slashing. Jesse grabbed one of the clubs he'd hidden and whacked the guard's arm. The man drew back with a yowl.

Emil rose from the floor like a whale breaching water. Jesse swung at him, but the man gripped the weapon and pulled hard. Jesse let his weight carry him down, landing on Emil's chest. His sharp features strangely calm, Emil struggled to gain control of the beam. Mouth curving, he slowly lifted all of Jesse's weight.

The guard grabbed Jesse around the neck, pulling him off Emil. "Louis was a friend of mine. Perhaps his silly little wife did not tell you."

Feet planted on the floor, Jesse pulled the guard's arm and tried to unbind the grip he had on him, exposing his middle in the process.

Emil struggled to his feet and drew back the club. Jesse braced for the hit that would probably break his ribs and pushed his feet into the floor, forcing his upper body into the hold. His head made contact with the guard's face. His grip slipped. Jesse turned to the side so the guard took the hit meant for him.

The man howled in pain. Jesse threw him to the floor, where he curled into a ball. Another club lay beside Aubrey's abandoned barrel. Jesse grasped it, facing Emil, who was ready with another swing of his club.

Jesse ducked. "Your brother was a coward, preying on one

weaker than him. There would be two babes if not for his foolishness."

Emil's expression flickered. "Louis's house was broken into the night before the marshal was given the files needed to arrest my brother. No one knew about those files but his wife, and you were in town to see her." Sweat wetted his brow. "I have a man who works for the police department. You broke into the house and gave him the files that sent my brother to prison—to his death." Emil darted left, then swung.

Jesse dodged and returned with a swing that laid the older man out. He kicked the club aside, panting.

Aubrey popped her head out from behind a bag of flour. "Watch the big one, Jesse!"

The guard lay inches from the door, holding his side. His knife was behind him, and a rope hung from his belt. Jesse kicked the knife away, then used the rope to bind Emil.

"He's getting away," Aubrey warned from the shadows.

Sure enough, the guard had gained his feet and was opening the door.

"He will lock us in!" Aubrey was helping again, and she wasn't wrong.

Jesse shoved a club between the frame and timber before the door slammed. Shouts sounded outside the room. Emil lay on his side, inhaling sips of air as he cradled his injured side, his face dark.

Gunshots fired somewhere far off. Footfalls thundered throughout the house. Had help arrived, or were more of Emil's men coming? Jesse raised his head out of the cellar for a second to see the main room. The way was dark with light coming through curtains into a room that might be a kitchen. The guard was heading around a table.

"Aubrey, hurry." Holding the club in one hand, he reached back for her.

She tiptoed her way over the flour sack, Emil, and finally,

the stone floor, where she slipped her hand into his. They tore into a dark kitchen, shadows hiding a movement in the corner. The guard he'd been chasing raised a rifle, pointing it at them. Behind the man, a door flew open and clobbered him in the head. He fell forward with a loud thump.

"Jesse!" Pa's shout filled the room. He tromped over the man. Then Pa was there wrapping his arms around them both.

Jesse dropped the club, and it landed with a clatter on the floor.

Pa's big laugh filled Jesse's ears and his heart. After weeks, he was reunited with his father, and if he was here, they must be safe.

Two policemen followed, one checking on the man Pa had knocked over with the door and the other lighting a lantern. The flame filled the room with a soft glow that reflected off Aubrey's cheeks when she peeked out from hugging Pa.

"Aubrey, what are you doing here?" Pa cupped Aubrey's face in his hands.

"They kidnapped me too. It's a long story. But how did you find us, Papa?" she asked in her old eager way.

Pa blinked and stumbled over a few words. "Well, it started with the telegraph from the Franklin sheriff saying that Jesse had been there but had disappeared in the middle of the night. I went there, anyway, looking for him. When his next telegram reached Sheriff Bernard, I was out with a pack of scouts looking for you. Bernard sent word to Idaho, though, and Abe Johnson was arrested when the authorities there found the gold. I still can't believe that man played me false." He growled through his teeth, then met Jesse's gaze. "Once I heard Jesse was at Salt Lake, I headed this way. Then tonight when I went to the hotel, Mrs. Shubert said you and your *wife* were missing."

"Wife?" Aubrey startled, then gave him a shove. "Jesse?"

"I can explain."

Pa shook his head. "No need. Mademoiselle Durand

showed up at the police station. Said Jesse told her to find Marshal Morris if anything went wrong. She knew where you were."

"Lorraine went to the police?" Was that after she followed Beau to the hideout house?

"Yes, sir. She was in pretty bad shape too." Pa's black eyebrows furrowed. He held Aubrey closer, only to push her back to arm's length and look down at her barrel-sized belly. "What is this?" A smile curled his mouth, then Aubrey started blubbering about the sins of the father, generational curses, and a mother's love. She was keeping her baby no matter what anyone said.

Jesse nearly covered her mouth before he grabbed his father's shoulder. "Pa—Lorraine? Where is she?"

"Now, son." Pa drew himself up to his full height. "You know that girl is wanted for murder."

"Is she safe?"

"Yes, they arrested her. She's at the jail. Safe."

His heart sank. Lorraine in a cell? She must be so distraught.

Marshal Morris came into the room. "Looks like a family reunion in here. All's well, Titus?"

"Yes, sir." Pa grinned, one arm still around Aubrey.

"The police rounded up a bunch of men. Added that man you laid out with the door to the bunch." He chuckled. "Haven't found that Emil character yet."

"Oh, he's in the cellar. Jesse beat him, then tied him, nice and tidy for you, Marshal Morris." Aubrey beamed despite leaning heavily on her father.

Pa's eyes widened, and Jesse's chest grew. Pa had never seen Jesse as tough, a fighter. Probably because he wasn't. He hated causing other people pain. He was even better at dodging punches than giving them, but that didn't mean he couldn't defend himself and others.

He wiped his palm onto his pants legs. "I'm going to see Lorraine." He started for the door, dodging a pair of men who were checking the house.

"Say, where did Deputy Andrew go?" one of the deputies asked as he and another deputy followed Marshal Morris to the cellar.

"You know, it's strange, but last I saw him, he was lagging behind the posse."

The deputy snorted. "I always said that Frenchman was yellow."

Jesse paused halfway up the steps, an ice-like chill on his neck.

"Andrew?" Aubrey spoke thoughtfully. "That's Andre in French. And didn't Emil say he had a man who worked for the police?"

Jesse turned, blood pounding through his veins so strongly he could hardly hear. "Pa, did you find a wiry little man named Pierre?"

"No, why?"

"Lorraine." Jesse charged through the door, one thought pushing him ahead. *Don't let them kill her, God.*

~

*L*orraine lay on the stinky cot in the dark, trying to force even breaths as she told herself that she was safe. This was America, not France. Monsieur Alexander and the other men had gone to rescue Jesse. That was what she wanted. He would be safe soon. They would come back and tell her what had happened.

Tobacco smoke floated in the air, stilling Lorraine's breath. No more than thirty minutes had passed since the men left without her. The rescue would take longer than that, so who was in the building?

The shadows of the jail closed in, light from the other room tipping into the doorway. A tall man obscured that bit of light, his pistol winged out from his holster.

Cold sweat broke across her neck, though Lorraine forced a slow inhale and sat up. "It would look suspicious if I was found dead in the cell."

"Indeed, mademoiselle." The tip of his cigarette glowed red. "But they won't find you in the cell, now, will they?" There was that glow again, and the scent grew stronger.

Deputy Andrew jingled a pair of keys as he stepped forward to unlock the door. It swung with a squeak. Lorraine held her wounded arm, muscles poised when he darted toward her. Just as she'd expected, he grabbed for her injured limb. She hooked her foot around his ankle, or maybe his calf—she couldn't tell in the darkness—but the resounding crash and swearing told her she'd been successful.

She raced out of the cell, then slammed the door. The lock clicked a moment before Andrew lunged against the bars like a rabid dog after prey. "Let me out, filthy petroleuse."

Lorraine stepped back in shock at the comment. "Petroleuse?" She'd not heard the term since the uprising in Paris. "Non, Deputy Andrew, I never burned anything. I was only a bystander, on neither side."

He answered in English, not even a hint of an accent. "Andre! My name is Andre."

Lorraine shuddered at his sudden outburst. "I did not take part in the fighting."

"Lies. Pierre told me you were a leader among the women arsonists. That even now, you send money to help the traitors still in prison."

"He lied. I did nothing. What does it matter to you, American?"

"I am French! My father was there! You killed him!" He shook the bars, though the keys were around his wrist. His teeth gnashed, then he reached through the bars, his fingers scraping her neck. "Filthy communard!"

Breath coming fast, Lorraine covered her mouth and shook her head. This poor man was still consumed over what had happened in Paris. Consumed with hate.

As though remembering he still held the key to her cell, he held the ring close to his face to inspect each key.

Lorraine turned, clambering through the police office straight into a man. She shouted and jerked away, but not before he shoved her. Unable to retain her balance, she crashed onto the hard floor, slamming the elbow of her good arm in the process.

Stars flashed across her vision. She rolled in pain, blind for a moment. Then two men were on her, one strapping a gag around her mouth and the other jerking her arms behind her back. She twisted and cried, only to be dragged across the floor.

God, help me. Help me! The only plea she could command with her mouth covered.

"Is there a back door?" Pierre's whisper sounded in the darkness.

What was he doing at the police station?

"This way," Andre responded, then they each hefted her by an arm and dragged her past a brick corner, a snoring prisoner, and farther into darkness.

A latch clicked. Once they cast her into the backyard, her fight would be lost. She had to get free. Lorraine dug her feet in the worn wooden floor. A back doorway opened with moonlight slipping in, and she was shoved through. Tripping on the threshold and unable to break her fall, she plunged forward, a silent scream held back by the gag. She squeezed her eyes shut against the impending impact.

But before she hit the ground, a strong pair of arms surrounded her. Large gentle hands caught her as though they'd been waiting. Her forehead scraped a whiskery chin, then the scent of soap and cedar encompassed her as Jesse held her—sheltering her.

One of the men yelped, then a gunshot exploded nearby. Ears ringing, Lorraine shuddered and pressed herself against Jesse, who now held her with one arm. A man shouted, but Lorraine didn't care. She hid from all that hurt and scared her. The crackle of a gun being cocked told her it had been Jesse who fired the shot and he wasn't done.

Pierre's curses sounded behind her, then the voice of the marshal telling him he was under arrest.

Jesse untied the gag, then freed her bonds. He ran a finger across the rope burns on her wrists and then to her cheek where the gag had cut in. Taking her hands, he kissed them, his soft breath fanning her skin. "I didn't think I'd make it in time." He closed his eyes. "Lorraine, if anything happened to you..."

She turned into the crook of his neck. "You made it. You saved me, mon amour."

He tensed, then cupped her chin and settled his lips upon hers with sweet urgency, as though there were not lawmen mere feet away, arresting those who had tried to kill her. "Somehow, it doesn't seem like so much is pitted against us anymore."

Leaning into him, she shook her head. "I'm still wanted for murder."

"Maybe not, missy." Marshal Morris stood in the doorway to the office, his hands on his hips. Blood pooled at his feet, and Lorraine hadn't the courage to ask if it belonged to Pierre or Andre, but his next words were a wonderful distraction. "I found them no-account Baker brothers in a barn on the property tied up. Once I got their gags off, they had plenty to say about Pierre Martin. Apparently, once Lorraine and Beau left with the gold, Pierre had the idea to kill a guard. He said the driver saw Lorraine, and she would be one less person to split the money with."

She shook her head, blinking her eyes. "Why would the Baker brothers confess so willingly?"

"I don't know, but they were in bad shape. Looked like both of them had taken a recent beating."

"Beau! It must be him. He knew I was in trouble and wanted to protect me. He probably beat them until they agreed to tell the truth." Not to mention, he had followed them to the barn that evening when Pierre and Emil went into the house.

Jesse blew through his lips. "I guess blessings come by many different means."

"Was Beau captured at the house as well?"

"I didn't see him, but you know he's wrong, Lorraine. If the law catches him, he'll reap what he's sown."

"I know." She couldn't be responsible for Beau's choices. He was a grown man.

Jesse took the handkerchief and gently wiped away the dirt from her cheeks. "I spent a good chunk of this night thinking about what I'd say if I ever saw you again." Heart thundering, she met his gaze. "God brought you into my life by extraordinary means. I didn't believe He would cause something like a kidnapping to work His good will, but He did. Since He's provided a way for you to be free, I'd like you to consider something more long term than a trip across the Utah-Idaho state line."

"Does that mean no more hiding in caves?" She let a smile play at her mouth.

"I'd rather go back and explore the cave, see where it leads to."

"Oh, we could go to Soda Springs and see the wells. And we could take Aubrey to Grays Lake."

"I think we might have to postpone that trip until next year, but there is one place I want to take you."

"Where is that?" She leaned against him and closed her eyes, her body hurting but her soul soaring.

"France. Paris, if you'd like. If what you say is true and you took no part in the rebellion, I think you can return safely. I have family there we could visit as well if you'd like."

Lorraine met his gaze with a start. "What? It's so far away."

"Only an ocean, but if you don't want to go, we don't have to."

She turned and wrapped her good arm around his neck, settling her lips on his for a few sweet moments.

Jesse cupped her jaw and smiled, caressing her cheek with his thumb. "Is that a yes to France?"

"That's yes to everything." And she kissed him again.

CHAPTER 16

MAY 1880
GRAYS LAKE, IDAHO

*L*orraine smiled as her little tot stumbled his way across the plot toward his papa. Jesse stood behind a tripod, his latest camera perched on the top. Little Jack grasped his pants and steadied himself.

Lorraine didn't need to see her son's face to know how he peered up with wide, cautious eyes, hiding behind his father's leg. Jack was so mild mannered, she sometimes feared for him. Who knew a male child could be so mellow? But then Jesse—despite his strength and courage—was calmer than most men she knew.

Sure enough, Jesse picked him up and threw the black cloth over both their heads so they could look into the lenses.

"I think Jesse will make a photographer out of Jack if you're not careful, Lorraine." Aubrey popped a cherry in her mouth, her fluffy white summer gown arrayed around her like clouds.

"A starving photographer. Won't Grandpa Alexander be proud?" Lorraine smiled, and her sister-in-law laughed.

There on the shore of Grays Lake stood Aubrey's children. Even from so far away, their little bodies trembled with anticipation as the man rowing to shore told them to wait. His laughter carried to where the two ladies lounged on a picnic blanket.

"Hurry before they dive in!" Aubrey shouted from cupped hands.

Her husband leapt from the boat and scooped them up, one in each arm. He then climbed back into the boat. They would go out to the middle and fish.

"Imagine if they hadn't waited. Those two will be the death of me. They are a wild pair, I tell you." She fell onto the quilt, crossing her arm over her face. "I don't know what I'd do on my own."

"Jesse is taking their photograph." Lorraine held the brim of her summer hat when a breeze tugged it.

"I don't know if we have enough room for more photographs. Did you see the studio he built?"

"Yes, a treasure trove of memories, and it all started with that one photograph of Grays Lake."

Aubrey beamed, peeking from beneath one arm. "We have taken the American Optical with us every summer for the last four years. Quite a collection, indeed."

"We could move some photographs to the cabin at Cariboo." Lorraine brushed back a strand of hair as cool mountain air swept peaceful arms around her.

Jesse carefully put away his equipment. He would spend hours in his developing studio once they returned to their home in Idaho. Soon, he approached with Jack holding his hand. The pudgy little boy used chubby legs to try and keep up with his pere. So precious.

Aubrey gazed to the faraway, snowy mountains where the sky touched the earth. "I think I could live here and be completely happy."

"Indeed." God had been good to Aubrey, and Lorraine, too, for that matter. She ran a hand over her swollen belly, the gentle fluttering there a promise of life. "I hope this one is a girl."

"Yes, it is high time we outnumbered the men again." Aubrey grinned cheekily.

The excited squeal of a child brought her attention up. Jack was pumping his arms, running with a large, drooly smile on his face.

At the opposite end of the field where the trees opened rode a man on a big black horse.

"Ah, Pa did decide to come." Aubrey gave him a wave just as Jesse reached the quilt.

He dropped down near Lorraine and slipped a pink wood rose behind her ear. "You are beautiful."

When she closed her eyes and sighed into his kiss, the warm sunlight dimmed.

By now, Jack had come close enough to the horse to pause amid tall, waving grass. Papa Alexander dismounted and approached cautiously with an outstretched hand. He lifted the tot so he could pet his horse and then climbed into the saddle. They rode forward together, Papa Alexander hugging the beaming boy.

"He's so gentle with Jack." Jesse's eyes lit with emotion.

Indeed, becoming a grandfather had softened the big, tough businessman.

When he reached them, he swung off his horse with Jack still in his arms. "Great news!" He thrust a newspaper toward Jesse and Lorraine.

She only glimpsed a few words, but they halted her breath. "Amnesty?"

Jesse read aloud how the French emperor, after much pressure from the people, had given total amnesty to all those who had been deported to New Caledonia. After years of Lorraine secreting supplies to the little island, paying off guards, writing petitions, and praying, the last of her people were free.

"Full amnesty." Jesse smiled down at her. "You did it, Lorraine."

"Nonsense. I was not the only one. We have had many generous supporters over the years."

Still, he shook his head, eyes full of pride.

"I don't understand." Aubrey sat up, propping herself with one arm. "Didn't the emperor already pardon people who hadn't committed violent crimes?"

"He did, but many people, including my neighbors and friends, were only ever suspected of supporting the Commune. Since they were never sentenced, the pardon did nothing for them."

"Unbelievable." Aubrey shook her head.

"It is sad." Papa Alexander looked down on her from his standing position where he held the horse so his grandson could pet it. "The Commune was not a republic by any means, but those folks have rights too."

"Yes, sir." Tears stung her eyes, and even if she'd not been with child, likely, they still would have come as she remembered the suffering of her people. Loved ones of her past.

"Desperate people do desperate things. I'm so glad God brought you out of it." Jesse squeezed Lorraine securely. He was always like that, there when she needed him.

The day wore on, fishing, snacking, making camp, and telling stories around the fire. Finally, they turned in, Lorraine to a down mattress covered by clean sheets where lay an already sleeping boy. Jesse shed his boots and curled up behind her, touching Jack's tummy gently and then Lorraine's, though the fluttering there was too soft for him to feel. His warm breath fanned her neck, and she found herself smiling. "You are my last thought before slumber."

"My last kiss before dreams." He spoke words they'd shared

on their honeymoon to France, promises of their love which had begun with such discord.

Safe in the arms of the man she loved with a babe tucked to her chest and one in her womb, Lorraine breathed a sigh. "Good night, mon amour."

THE END

Did you enjoy this book? We hope so!
Would you take a quick minute to leave a review where you purchased the book?
It doesn't have to be long. Just a sentence or two telling what you liked about the story!

Receive a FREE ebook and get updates when new Wild Heart books release: https://wildheartbooks.org/newsletter

SNEAK PEEK: THE BOUNTY HUNTER'S SURRENDER

Don't miss the next book in the Outlaw Hearts series!

The Bounty Hunter's Surrender

JUNE 1875
A FEW MILES OUTSIDE SAN FRANCISCO

He had no business being in her house, and yet here he was, his snakeskin boots setting softly on the rug before the moonlit desk as he slid off the windowsill. Bounty hunter Nathan Reed navigated his way forward, the wooden surface smooth beneath his fingertips.

His hand bumped something glass, and...

No!

It tumbled and hit the floor.

Nathan's heart thundered. He shifted back, one hand on the windowsill lest he needed a quick escape. All was quiet, inside the house and out where a garden sat in cool moonlit hues.

What was he doing, breaking and entering? He'd always worked within the bounds of the law, but everything was different with this assignment. Not that he could have turned down Ellsworth and the large sum he'd offered. Nathan was providing for more than just himself now.

Lord, have I made a huge mistake?

It was too late to back out.

Though man's laws would condemn him, he felt no conviction in his spirit, so he reached into his pocket and withdrew a match. He struck it on the tip of his thumbnail, and the end blossomed into a bright flame. The desk held only an inkwell, stacks of paper, the knocked-over glass, pencils, and quills. He pulled out the drawers, one at a time, not entirely surprised to find them empty. Barely a home, the house included few personal items. Just basic furniture.

The light on the end of his match wavered. He needed a lamp. If he lit the wick and turned it low, he could see the paperwork and likely still go undetected. The staff members here were old, and the lady of the house slept in a different wing. The last thing he wanted was to come across the Widow Willot.

Pulling out another match, he surveyed his surroundings. The room was expansive yet eerily empty, considering the size. Two wingback chairs and a sofa faced the fireplace. Most of the towering bookshelves were bare, the expensively carved woodwork glowing.

Nathan spotted a lamp on a side table near the sofa and crossed the space. His faint light shone on letters scattered on the rug in front of the sofa. The penmanship was familiar. The letters had been written by Louis Willot, and judging by the content, they were personal letters to his wife, not the business documents he was looking for. Creases marked the pages as though Mrs. Willot had crumpled and then smoothed them out again.

The woman would be better off tossing them into the fireplace than pondering them. If she knew of the letters written to Nathan's own sister, she would know they weren't worth keeping.

There was a movement to his left. His gaze landed on a woman slumbering on the sofa. Brown curls cascaded across the upholstery. He could make out her gently sloped nose and lips. A white cotton nightgown hugged her very round stomach.

The Widow Willot.

A thousand horses raced in his chest, and his feet felt staked onto the floor. What was she doing in the study?

And she was expecting a child?

A faint moan escaped her lips, and she caressed her belly.

Pain singed his finger. He shook the match out and sank behind the sofa. The rustle of fabric stilled him.

Had she awakened? Would the darkness of the room cloak him sufficiently enough for him to go unnoticed? If she hadn't already glimpsed him when the match was lit.

"There, *mon tresor*." She uttered the words in a sleepy, feminine voice, then rose. The mirror above the mantel reflected her figure, ethereal in the moonlight.

Nathan halted, scarcely breathing as he prayed she wouldn't see him.

Yawning, she stretched out a hand and started toward him.

He didn't dare move, even when her gown dragged across his leg.

She froze, likely feeling the tug.

He was done for.

He braced for her scream, but she scampered away, the door thudding gently on her exit.

Nathan hastened to the window. He lifted the latch, climbed through, and landed in a boxwood hedge, which sent him stumbling to the side. His foot caught in a hole so that his ankle twisted sharply. Pain radiated through the bone. Sucking in a breath, he pulled the window shut, then stepped away. His foot failed, and he bent with his hands on his knees, just breathing for a moment.

What a fool he'd been to break in when she was home. Despite his caution to avoid her bedroom and choose a late hour, he'd still almost been caught. He should have waited for her to leave the house. She had to have sensed him, which meant she'd be more cautious in the future. The risk of getting caught was higher now—but he had to find those documents.

The window he'd just jumped through glowed. Nathan plastered himself to the side of the building.

"Where are you?" Mrs. Willot's tone carried a strong note of warning from within the room, though it sounded as though she was on the far side. "I have a gun, and I will shoot you."

He crouched lower beneath the windowsill.

Except for the leaves whispering on a peach tree, the night was calm.

A crash came from inside...across the room he'd exited.

Had she fallen? Nathan peeked over the sill.

Mrs. Willot held a lantern and revolver before one of the bookcases—with the entire piece of furniture pulled away, revealing an opening. Behind it, a table and a vase of flowers lay on the floor. That must've been the cause of the crash.

"Who's in there?" She held the gun shakily, her back to Nathan. "Louis?"

Nathan backed away.

May the good Lord grant him forgiveness. He had erred in coming this night and giving Mrs. Willot such a fright. Why had she called for her dead husband? Had she in her weary state forgotten he died? It was a recent death. Just two weeks.

He'd searched the remainder of the house before she moved to town and found nothing. The documents Ellsworth wanted, must be in the passage way. It was just a shame he'd likely discovered the whereabouts of the documents, at Mrs. Willot's expense. She had, doubtlessly, suffered at the hands of her husband when he lived. Now Nathan intruded upon the sanctity of her home. In doing so, had he resurrected old ghosts?

Mrs. Willot slammed the secret door hard enough that a few books toppled to the floor. Her gaze landed on the letters scattered over the table. Weapon thrust aside, she grasped the pages and ripped them to tiny pieces. Then, as if weakened by the action, she sank onto the velvet settee and cupped her face. "Lord, am I going mad?"

He sighed and bowed his head, imagining God looking down past the stars and cloud-skirted moon to Nathan in the hedges and the widow on the sofa while both prayed for help.

Nathan had hunted Louis Willot, determined to make the man pay for his folly, but the miscreant had died in prison before Nathan found an opportunity to confront him. Still, there had to be remuneration for the loss.

His ankle still throbbing, Nathan limped past the French garden with its many square beds and a fountain in the center. All too aware of his vulnerable position, he hurried across a field toward the carriage house on grass still soft from spring rains. On the edge of the property, a grove of trees offered welcome shelter, but Nathan did not slow his stride until he saw his horse.

"Reed?" His friend Beau emerged from the woods like a mystic.

Nathan wasn't surprised to find the Frenchman so close to the house. His skill set made him the perfect lookout. What the man lacked in confidence, he made up for in stealth.

"Were you seen?" His thickly accented voice carried in the night.

"No. But nearly." Nathan untied his horse. "I am done for now. Did you know she was pregnant?"

When his friend remained as still as the surrounding trees, Nathan let the matter drop, and they headed for San Francisco. The miles were haunted by the burden of having frightened the pregnant widow. Her condition complicated things.

At last, they reached the city and parted ways. When Nathan rode up to the bakery, the typical feelings of inadequacy weighed heavily on him. If he'd made better life choices, lived for someone other than himself, he might be better suited to provide for his sweet little niece. Despite the late hour, the baker was preparing tomorrow's bread, and light shone from the upstairs apartment.

Nathan tiptoed up the stairs to where a frowning Mrs. Andrews bid him enter. Inside the apartment, he hastened to the dresser drawer that served as a makeshift cradle.

Inside slept a baby whose hair was as light as fresh butter. Barely able to breathe, Nathan cradled Felicity in his arms, supporting her head even though Mrs. Andrews said she was strong enough to manage on her own. She yawned, her tiny pink mouth opening to reveal her tongue, then she continued to sleep.

He was taking no chances with this little golden-haired angel. He needed a steady income—something more reliable than bounty hunting—to raise a child. Not to mention, Felicity needed a mother, not a nurse. He also had to right the wrongs done to Felicity and her mother.

Nathan lowered himself into a rocking chair near a window and tipped back, setting the chair into motion. His mind turned over all he had seen at the Willot Château—the secret door and the pregnant widow.

This second babe changed everything.

ABOUT THE AUTHOR

KyLee Woodley is a cheery romantic who loves to write about bygone days and heartwarming romance with a pinch of adventure. She teaches preschool at a lab school in Texas, where she lives with her husband of eighteen years and their three teenage children. On weekends, KyLee cohosts and produces the Historical Bookworm Show, a steadily growing author interview podcast for history lovers and readers of historical fiction.

In her spare time, she cares for a rescue mutt named Lucky, a feisty feline named Hazel, and two adorable Boston Terrier puppies. She listens to Cricket Country and K-Love radio, reads classic books with her children, and watches Marvel movies with her husband, who might resemble Superman

AUTHOR'S NOTE

Dear Reader,

I hope you enjoyed Lorraine and Jesse's love story. Their journey—both figuratively and literally—was one full of unexpected twists that were a joy for me to discover. Thank you for joining me!

Here are some fun historical tidbits for you history lovers. Caribou Mountain in Idaho (called Cariboo in the story because that was the name in historical documents at the time) was named after a miner called Jesse Fairchild, also known as Cariboo Jack. He spent time mining in the Caribou Mountains in British Columbia and earned the name Cariboo Jack because of the tall tales he told regarding his adventures there. Jesse discovered gold in what is now the Caribou Mountains area just north of Grays Lake, Idaho. This area was mined into the early 1900s. Eventually, the name was changed to Caribou like the animal.

I had so much fun researching the historical side of Lorraine's past including the Château d'Écouen—a school for the daughters of less prestigious French military officers. Lorraine's father was a soldier, and so she qualified to attend.

To do this, she had to leave her mother who was a Roma or Romani (*gypsy* is slang and considered vulgar and insulting). The Romani people were typically nomadic, traveling from place to place and sometimes camping outside Paris.

The Bloody Week occurred shortly after the Franco-Prussian War. Paris had been besieged by the Prussian army during which time privation ravaged the city. Parisians' lives did not improve when their government signed the armistice with Germany. The French government rescinded the wartime moratorium on debt repayment, crippling the working class of Paris whose industry and commerce had stalled during the war. A revolt rose up in Paris, spearheaded by a group known as the Paris Commune, and was put down during the Bloody Week— May 21-27, 1871. The death toll is not known and has been debated by historians for years. It is certain to be in the thousands. Some members of the Commune who survived were sentenced to death, imprisoned, or sent to penal colonies. One of these was New Caledonia in Australia. Years later, pardons were given; however, since a number of people had been imprisoned without trial or conviction, these pardons were only for those with actual documentation. Finally, in the 1880s, a general amnesty was granted, allowing the remaining condemned to return to France if they so desired. Lorraine's part in this was purely fictional.

I would be ever so grateful if you would post a review of *The Bandit's Redemption* on Amazon.

Praying for blessings and inspiration in your reading-life.

~ KyLee

For new releases and special promotions, subscribe to KyLee Woodley's mailing list: https://KyLeeWoodley.com

ACKNOWLEDGMENTS

Firstly, and always, I thank God for guiding my life and gifting me with the call to write. For a woman who was practically illiterate at the age of fifteen, this is a testimony to His miracle-working greatness. You said to write stories for You, and here is the first of—Lord willing—many. As long as You provide, I will continue. Secondly, thank you to my children and husband who have believed in me and supported me over the years. I do not deserve such confident cheerleaders.

Many writers from American Christian Fiction Writers have supported me and my work for years, but for this book, a special thanks to Kelly Borjas, Christie Kern, and Darcy Fornier for reading the entire manuscript. Christie, thank you for your blunt and needed recommendations. You even read it twice! Many thanks, my friend. Karissa Riffel Fisher, Stephanie Goddard, and L. Cecil, thank you for critiquing chapters of this work. I hope you enjoy the final product!

To my sister KayDee, thank you for your continuous belief in me. You were the first person I let read my work. No matter how terrible those first drafts were, you encouraged and supported me. I love you, sister!

To the team at Wild Heart Books, thank you for your dedication to excellence, especially my editors Barbar Curtis and Denise Weimer. Your thoroughness, kindness, and exceptional editorial skills are invaluable to me.

WANT MORE?

If you love historical romance, check out the other Wild Heart books!

Lone Star Ranger by Renae Brumbaugh Green

Elizabeth Covington will get her man.

And she has just a week to prove her brother isn't the murderer Texas Ranger Rett Smith accuses him of being. She'll show the good-looking lawman he's wrong, even if it means setting out on a risky race across Texas to catch the real killer.

Rett doesn't want to convict an innocent man. But he can't let the Boston beauty sway his senses to set a guilty man free. When Elizabeth follows him on a dangerous trek, the Ranger vows to keep her safe. But who will protect him from the woman whose conviction and courage leave him doubting everything—even his heart?

～

Murmur in the Mud Caves by Kathleen Denly

He came to cook for ranch hands, not three single women.

Gideon Swift, a visually impaired Civil War Veteran, responds
to an ad for a ranch cook in the Southern California desert
mountains. He wants nothing more than to forget his past and
stay in the kitchen where he can do no harm. But when he
arrives to find his employer murdered, the ranch turned to
ashes, and three young women struggling to survive in the
unforgiving Borrego Desert, he must decide whether his presence protects them or places them in greater danger.

Bridget "Biddie" Davidson finally receives word from her older
sister who disappeared with their brother and pa eighteen
years prior, but the news is not good. Determined to help her
family, Biddie sets out for a remote desert ranch with her
adopted father and best friend. Nothing she finds there is as
she expected, including the man who came to cook for the
shambles of a ranch.

When tragedy strikes, the danger threatens not only her plans to help her sister, but her own dreams for the future—with the man who's stolen her heart.

~

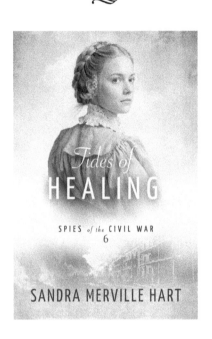

Tides of Healing by Sandra Merville Hart

A Southern belle fights to reclaim her home, but will her spying destroy the Union officer she never meant to love?

Savannah Adair has endured the unimaginable, hiding in a cave while her beloved Vicksburg was under siege. With the city now occupied by Union soldiers, Savannah cannot stand by and do nothing. So when one of the gaunt, half-starved Confederate prisoners asks her to spy for the South, she can't refuse the chance to take back her home.

First Lieutenant Travis Lawson takes pride in the Union army's hard-fought victory, but he quickly realizes that the challenges of rebuilding and reconciliation are just beginning . . . and not everyone is appreciative of changes he's making. Namely, the fiery and alluring Savannah Adair. Despite their differing loyalties and the societal divide between them, Travis cannot deny the growing feelings he has for her. When he is tasked with finding Southern spies in Vicksburg and he captures a female spy, Travis is forced to consider that the woman he's beginning to love may be the enemy.

www.ingramcontent.com/pod-product-compliance
Lightning Source LLC
LaVergne TN
LVHW011208250125
802092LV00007B/180